Tom Becker

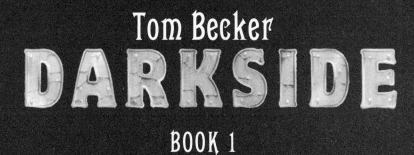

# DARKSIDE

## BOOK 1

Orchard Books
New York
An Imprint of Scholastic Inc.

All rights reserved. Published by Orchard Books, an imprint of Scholastic
Inc., *Publishers since 1920*, 557 Broadway, New York, New York 10012, by
arrangement with Scholastic Ltd. ORCHARD BOOKS and design are registered
trademarks of Watts Publishing Group, Ltd., used under license. SCHOLASTIC
and associated logos are trademarks and/or registered trademarks of
Scholastic Inc.

ISBN-13: 978-0-545-03739-6
ISBN-10: 0-545-03739-5

Library of Congress Cataloging-in-Publication Data
Becker, Tom.
Darkside / Tom Becker.—1st ed.
p.  cm.— (Darkside ; bk. 1)
Summary: Jonathan Starling's father is in an asylum and his home has been
attacked when, while running away from kidnappers, he stumbles upon
Darkside, a terrifying and hidden part of London ruled by the descendents
of Jack the Ripper, where Jonathan is in mortal danger if he cannot find the
way out.
ISBN-13: 978-0-545-03739-6 (reinforced lib. bdg.)
ISBN-10: 0-545-30739-5 (reinforced lib. bdg.) [1. Supernatural—Fiction.
2. London (England)—Fiction. 3. Horror stories.] I. Title.
PZ7.B3817177Dar        2008
[Fic]—dc22

2007023634

10 9 8 7 6 5 4 3 2          08 09 10 11

Printed in the U.S.A.

Reinforced Binding for Library Use

First edition, February 2008

This edition designed by Phil Falco

For Mum, Dad, and Meirionwen,
who filled my childhood with stories

# Prologue

Ricky Thomas wished that he had never gotten out of bed. He wished that his mom hadn't bothered to wake him up early that morning, and that he'd missed the bus. His class went racing through the subway passage, screaming and whooping like some savage prehistoric tribe. One of the bigger guys shoved past Ricky, smacking him in the face with his bag. Ricky stumbled and stepped into a puddle, sending a stream of cold water splashing over his jeans. The boy turned around and grinned.

"Watch your step, fat boy!" he crowed.

Perfect. This day was getting better and better.

Up ahead, the passage curved away from him. The shouts and squeals of the students ricocheted off the walls, filling the subway with raucous noise. A small platoon of teachers struggled to subdue their rowdy pupils. Hanging back from the others, Ricky dabbed at the puddle stain with a tissue, but only succeeded in turning the tissue black. He stuffed it back into his pocket and thought wistfully of his bed.

The subway ended in a set of steep steps, and the class emerged into the early-autumn morning. Ricky shivered and drew the hood of his jacket tighter around his face. The sky was gray and swollen with rain. It was bitingly cold. They were standing on the edge of a vast square, cut off from the rest of the world by broad, busy lanes of traffic. Despite the early hour, there was already a scattering of tourists milling around the huge fountains. Pigeons scratched at the ground. On top of a column far above everyone's head, a statue gazed solemnly out over the streets and rooftops of London, as stark and lonely as a lighthouse.

Mr. Watkins, a balding history teacher with a harassed expression etched permanently onto his face, clapped his hands together and addressed the group. "Right, listen up. Listen! We have arrived at Trafalgar Square. Now follow me, and for heaven's sake don't go wandering off anywhere. Darren? That goes for you too." Behind his back, a boy aimed a wild kick at a pigeon. It fluttered away a few feet, and then resumed pecking at something on the pavement.

The group trudged dispiritedly toward a small statue of a man named Henry Havelock, and Mr. Watkins began reciting facts and figures about some rebellion that had happened in some other country years and years ago. Ricky let the dates wash over him, and stared up at Havelock's grim, unblinking face. He wondered what sort of person you had to be to fight in battle, to risk your life, and to kill people. Normally Ricky wouldn't harm a fly, but occasionally a splinter of rage pricked his insides, rage against the kids who picked on him and the teachers who ignored him. Whenever he got that fierce look in his eyes, his mom would sigh and say he'd inherited his dad's temper. Ricky wouldn't know — he had never met him.

A particularly inquisitive pigeon had pecked too close to Darren again. This time Mr. Watkins spotted him lashing out. "And what do you think you're doing?" he roared. "Come to the front here where I can see you! If you're going to act like a child, I'm going to treat you like one!"

Taking advantage of the commotion, Ricky slipped away from the rest of the class and headed for the opposite side of the square. He knew that Mr. Watkins would be shouting for some time, so he might as well sit down. He walked past a fountain on his left-hand side and trailed a hand through its icy pool. The wind had wrested control of the jets of water, and the spray, instead of going straight up in the air, flew crazily to one side like an old man's comb-over. Ricky skirted around the wet patch on the pavement and found a bench by the wall. From here he figured he could keep an eye on his classmates and rejoin them before they left the square.

Ricky's stomach rumbled angrily. He'd already polished off the sandwiches his mom had made for him on the way down. The girls sitting behind him had sniggered and whispered to each other at seeing him rooting around in his bag, but Ricky didn't care. He was used to being laughed at. It almost didn't bother him anymore. Surprisingly, an old chocolate bar had escaped his attention and was lying at the bottom of his bag. He brushed a bit of fuzz from the wrapper and took a contented bite.

Mr. Watkins was having trouble keeping everyone together. On the other side of the square, a gaggle of girls squealed as a fountain splashed them, while two boys were attempting to clamber up one of the bronze lions that slumbered at the base of Nelson's Column. They didn't notice him. Watching everyone disperse, Ricky wondered why the teachers had bothered to bring them here.

It had started to spit with rain, and the wind whistled in his ears, carrying with it a strong scent of women's perfume. He was going to get soaked. Ricky's skin prickled slightly with alarm, and he had the sudden sensation that someone was looking back at him. Had one of the teachers spotted him? He hurriedly scanned the square. To his left there was a group of foreign students, jabbering at one another in a language he didn't understand, and then a street sweeper in a fluorescent jacket, and then a young Japanese couple taking photographs of each other, and then . . .

Ricky stopped. In the midst of the crowd there was a tall, shadowy figure, his head and shoulders towering far above everyone else like a dark skyscraper. His hair was slicked down and he was dressed in a black suit and waistcoat that gave him the appearance of an undertaker. There was no expression on his face, but one thing was clear: He was staring directly at Ricky. As they made eye contact, Ricky felt dizzy, and all the crowds and the cars and the buildings around him began to melt away, to be replaced by a swirling, suffocating darkness. With effort he tore his gaze away from the man and looked down at his feet, trying to catch his breath. When he brought his head back up, the man was still staring at him.

In the distance, the remnants of the class still listening to Mr. Watkins had moved away from the statue of Henry Havelock, and were now clustered around Nelson's Column. Ricky gathered up his things and began walking in their direction. The tall man saw him go, and stepped forward after him. Without looking up, the foreign students eased out of the way to form a path, as if they could feel his presence but could not see him. Ricky started to walk a little faster.

The undertaker moved slowly and with great deliberation. He appeared to be in no hurry. A grin of reptilian anticipation had spread across his face. There seemed to be a faint blur around him, a smudge of gray, and people stepped out of his way like sleepwalkers. Who was this guy? What did he want with him?

Ricky glanced over his shoulder, and the man nodded

in the direction of the column. He followed his gaze. Another undertaker. Small and sharp-faced, this man, dressed in an identical black suit, had stepped in between Ricky and the rest of his class. He was completely bald, and a long, narrow nose dominated his face. Unlike his companion, this undertaker couldn't stop moving, bouncing on his heels with excitement as he muttered to himself. Seeing the boy heading toward him, he pointed at him and slowly drew a finger across his throat, as if he were slicing it with a knife.

Ricky shouted over to the rest of his class, "Mr. Watkins! Over here! Help!" His voice was swallowed up by the wind and the crashing fountains. As the two men advanced upon him from either side, he tugged the sleeve of a man in an anorak standing next to him — "Hey, mister! Mister!" — but the man didn't even look up. It was as if Ricky had become invisible. This couldn't be happening to him. Maybe he hadn't left his bed after all, and this was all one horrible nightmare. His heart was pounding in his chest, and tears of fear stung his eyes.

No one was going to help him here; he had to move. Ricky made for the top left corner of the square, where there was a broad flight of stone stairs offering an escape route out. As he skipped up the stairs, he knocked into the young Japanese couple that had been taking photographs nearby. He apologized over his shoulder, but they didn't even react. At the top of the stairs, Ricky turned right. The two undertakers were side by side now, following him up the steps. The smaller man hopped from one foot to the other, impatient at his taller companion's slow, deliberate gait.

Ricky looked left at the big, grand building looming ominously over him. Banners advertising some sort of art exhibition flapped in the wind. In front of him stood an old church, its spire standing proudly upright against the skyline. Surely he would be safe in there, if he could just make it inside. The green man faded away on the pedestrian sign just as, behind him, the smaller man cackled and strained forward. Ricky jabbed the button on the traffic lights, but the cars swept past him. They were only a few paces behind him now. There was nothing to do. . . .

Ricky darted across the road, narrowly avoiding a car that beeped with fury. He scampered triumphantly up to the church. A painted sign on the side of the building declared that it was the church of St.-Martins-in-the-Field. Risking a glance back, Ricky saw that his two pursuers were still waiting on the other side of the road. The smaller man was jittery with anger, but the taller man merely grinned. Ricky shuddered and ran through the church doors.

Inside it was blissfully quiet. The wind and the rain and the traffic were reduced to a soft hum. Ricky pushed his hood down and went forward, gazing upward at the ornate roof. The pews were empty, except for a young woman sitting in the front row. She was dressed in a long crimson dress and hat, and her head was bowed in prayer. As Ricky shuffled into the row behind her, he caught sight of a couple of strands of dyed fluorescent orange hair escaping from the bottom of her hat.

The pew creaked as he sat down, and she turned around at the noise. Though there was not a drop of color in her pale face, she was beautiful. Her eyes were filled with tears. "Hello," she said gravely.

"Uh . . . hi." He paused. "Are you OK?"

She smiled and wiped at her eyes with the back of her hand. "I'll be OK. Thank you for asking."

"S'all right."

Despite her sadness, her voice was light and melodious. Ricky scratched his head, unsure of what to do. The woman patted the seat next to her affectionately and he moved around next to her. He was dimly aware that the sweet scent he had smelled in the square had returned.

"So why are you here?" she asked gently. "You look unhappy, just like me."

Behind him, the wind slammed a door shut, and Ricky whirled around. There was no one there. He was being stupid. He had to calm down. "Yeah . . . I'm all right now. Just some people picking on me."

The woman sighed. "People can be so mean to one another."

Ricky shifted uncomfortably in the wooden seat. "Can I ask you a question?" he said finally.

"Of course, my dear."

"Why were you crying when I came in?"

She sighed softly. "It's complicated."

"You don't have to tell me. . . ."

"No. It's fine. It's just that I get upset when I have to take one of the little ones."

Back in the square, Mr. Watkins was looking forward to getting out of the blasted rain and having a cup of tea, but there was a problem with the head count.

"No, we're definitely one short. I've counted twice."

Mr. Watkins sighed. There was always one.

"We saw Ricky Thomas going out of the square," someone piped up.

The teacher looked around. That was just great. The boy could be anywhere. Why did they have to do this to him? He cupped his hands together. "Ricky!" he shouted.

Outside the church of St.-Martins-in-the-Field, a group of people were getting into a black van with HUMBLE & SKEET UNDERTAKINGS painted onto the side. One of them looked very unsteady on his feet and had to be helped into the van. An extremely tall man folded himself carefully into the driver's seat, and the vehicle moved away. High above them all, Lord Nelson maintained his silent, impassive vigil.

# 1

They were building down by the banks of the Thames, and the air shook with the rumble of diggers and the insistent drumbeat of drills. Men in hard hats and fluorescent jackets tramped around on the sand, shouting at one another through cupped hands. Spindly cranes poked up on the horizon like drinking straws. At the moment the site looked like a battlefield, scarred with holes and rubble, but in a few months, a year maybe, there would be another huge building reaching proudly up toward the heavens. It was as if the city had decided that there was no room for it to spread on the ground and was now trying to construct a new civilization way up in the sky.

Jonathan Starling leaned on the rails and watched the men as they worked, his jacket shivering in the breeze. He was a gangly fourteen-year-old with unruly brown hair that shot off in unexpected directions. His gray eyes had a haunted tint to them, and every movement he made said *leave me alone*. Concealed beneath his jacket, his school uniform was a size too small for him and clung awkwardly to his body.

That was how a stranger might have described him, but if you had asked the people who knew Jonathan what he looked like, they would have struggled for a reply. They might have instinctively frowned or shrugged, but he just wasn't the sort of person other people took much notice of. (Then again, if you had asked Jonathan what he looked like, he wouldn't have been able to answer either. He hadn't looked in a mirror for years.)

This ability to escape attention — to disappear from sight — had come in handy over the years. It had allowed him to slip out of school without the hassle of parental notes and the suspicious inquisitions of his teachers. Instead he slipped through the front gates like a ghost and was gone. When he should have been dozing through a chemistry lesson, or halfheartedly dragging his mud-splattered legs around the sports field, he wandered the streets of London, in search of something different.

He explored the winding alleyways of Soho, picked his way through the tangled mossy graves at Highgate Cemetery, while up by Alexandra Palace he looked down on the sprawling ants' nest that was his city.

Jonathan didn't always get away with it. There were truant officers and policemen combing the streets, and particularly observant teachers who noticed his empty chair in class. From time to time he would find himself in the principal's office, sitting quietly as she shook her head sadly and gave him encouraging speeches. He had been suspended several times and was now on his last warning. At least he never got into any trouble at home for it. The school had tried to bring his dad in on several occasions, and Jonathan was always careful that they received a convincing — but negative — reply. He sometimes told them that his dad was too ill to attend; and sometimes, at least, that was true.

That day the prospect of math class had seemed too much to cope with, and Jonathan had slipped out of the school's back gate during lunch. As he was crossing London Bridge, the gleaming superstructures of Canary Wharf had caught his eye. He caught a tube train on the Jubilee Line and headed down there, making sure not to catch anyone's eye as they rattled along the Underground. By the time he had arrived it was midafternoon, and there were dark smudges at the edge of the cold, bright autumn sky. The broad streets and squares were still busy with people hurrying from one place to another. They kept their heads down, as if cowed by the monstrous glass buildings that reared up on all sides.

In the distance, Jonathan made out the familiar silhouette of a policeman walking down the access road toward him. It was time to move. If they started asking questions, you were done for. Trying to look as casual as possible, he walked away from the rail and headed back between two buildings toward the center of the wharf. The policeman shouted something at him but he pretended not to hear. As soon as he was around the corner, he took off in a run.

Jonathan might not have broken any records on the athletic track, but in a chase through London streets he was untouchable. He zigzagged past office workers and shoppers, cutting through a small green park where people were ice-skating around a makeshift rink. They twirled and flowed in graceful arcs as Jonathan raced past them. He heard the policeman shout again, but it was a long way back and he was losing ground all the time. Jonathan ignored the entrance to a vast shopping center, preferring to stick to the open spaces. Shopping centers had surveillance cameras and security guards and were always on the lookout for kids stealing stuff. He was safer out here.

He crossed a couple of streets and found himself in a small square. A fountain tossed soothing splashes of water into the air. On the corner a small kiosk was selling coffee and snacks. The roads around the square were quiet, and there was a sense of stillness about the place that reassured Jonathan. Glancing around, he could see that he had lost the policeman. He was safe for now. He settled down on a marbled wall and caught his breath.

On one side of the square three massive buildings soared high above him, standing shoulder to shoulder beneath the clouds. The largest one was in the middle, and at its summit a light flashed on and off to warn low-flying planes of its presence. Just craning his neck up to see it made Jonathan feel small and insignificant. He wondered what it must be like to work on the top floor, to spend every day looking down on the rest of the world.

It was then that the woman caught his eye. She was jauntily crossing the square, clad in a pinstriped suit and tapping an umbrella on the ground as she went. A bowler hat was perched elegantly on one side of her head, allowing a cascade of fluorescent pink hair to fall away. Although no one else seemed to have noticed her, there was something about the woman that mesmerized Jonathan and made it very difficult to take his eyes off her. She saw him watching her, and gave him a broad grin. Changing direction midstride, she began to head toward him, sending a ripple of sensation down Jonathan's skin that was as unsettling as it was unexplainable.

At the same time, the policeman entered the square from the other side, huffing and puffing and red-faced from his exertions. Jonathan got up slowly and began to edge away toward the exit. Seeing his pursuer, the woman winked at Jonathan and put a finger over her lips. She then approached the policeman and began to ask him a long-winded question. Jonathan didn't need a second invitation — he turned and ran. Whoever that woman was, she had done him a big favor.

He was nearing the tube station when his phone began ringing in his pocket, making him jump. He fumbled around for it and checked the caller display. It was Mrs. Elwood — their next-door neighbor, and his dad's only friend. That could only mean one thing. Bad news.

"Hello?"

"Hi, Jonathan. It's me. Look . . . your dad's fallen ill again. They've taken him to the hospital. I'm going to drive there now. Are you still at school? I'll pick you up on the way."

Jonathan looked around. Rows and rows of windows stared blankly back at him. "No, it's all right. I'm on my way home," he said.

# 2

Mrs. Elwood tapped her fingers on the steering wheel with impatience. "Oh, this construction! Nothing's moving tonight. I'm afraid the journey's going to take forever." She reached down to the glove compartment and extracted a couple of rather ancient candies from the clutter. "Want one?"

Jonathan shook his head. "I'm OK."

Mrs. Elwood smiled, and gave him a quick pat on the arm. She was a tiny woman, perhaps only four feet five inches, with long blonde hair that reached down and tickled her waist. She needed to sit on a cushion to see over the steering wheel, and the pedals had been specially adapted to allow her feet to make contact with them. The first time he had ridden in a car with her, this unusual setup had made Jonathan feel very nervous. That had been years ago. Now he knew that Mrs. Elwood was a fast, smooth driver: not a woman to be underestimated.

"I was watching the news before you turned up," she said, chewing thoughtfully on a toffee. "A boy your age has gone missing on a school trip. In Trafalgar Square. And in broad daylight, too! His parents must be going crazy with worry."

Jonathan grunted. He wanted to turn on the radio, but he knew that she wanted to talk to him, to try and make him feel better. As always when his dad was ill, Jonathan was struggling with how to react. He felt that everyone expected, almost *wanted* him to be crying and wailing with anxiety. But then Alain Starling had been ill so many times, and Jonathan had spent so many hours waiting in drafty hospital corridors, that he didn't really have the strength to feel anything anymore. This was just . . . what happened.

"How did you find out about Dad?" he asked.

"I saw the ambulance going past from my front window. I had a horrible premonition it was for him. So I went outside and saw it parked outside your house." She sighed. "Oh, it's such a shame, Jonathan. I thought he'd been doing much better recently. He seemed more like his old self."

Jonathan shrugged. He didn't really know what his dad's "old self" was like. Alain had been distant and remote with his son for as long as he could remember. But then, Jonathan knew that Mrs. Elwood had known his dad for a long time, long enough to remain his friend after everyone else had gone away. Maybe he had been different back then.

She was right about one thing, though. It had been a while since his dad had gotten sick. Everyone had different names for what happened: Neighbors described them as *turns* or *episodes*; doctors used a variety of incredibly long and complex medical terms to hide the fact that they didn't know what was going on; the kids in his school simply said he'd gone nuts. Jonathan preferred to use the word his dad had whispered in his ear once, in a rare moment of clarity. "The darkening, son. I can feel the darkening. . . ."

The cars in front of them slowly began to move. Mrs. Elwood patted Jonathan on the arm again and smiled. "It'll be all right, you know. Do you want the radio on?"

Jonathan nodded, and they didn't say another word to each other until they reached the hospital.

Like a medieval monastery, St. Christopher's Hospital was sheltered from the outside world, behind a high wall in an area toward the west of the city, near Hyde Park. It was a place for the long-term ill and the mentally disturbed: There was no Emergency Room here. Although the narrow hallways smelled of disinfectant just like every other hospital, the place was infused with a different, otherworldly atmosphere. Jonathan felt it as soon as the car passed under the arches and into the parking lot: a pervasive air of hopelessness.

Evening was rapidly descending upon them, and as Jonathan got out of the car he felt a couple of raindrops patter onto his head. He headed through the automatic doors and into the hospital. There was no general reception area, and no one in view, but Jonathan immediately began striding down the nearest hallway. A left turn, and then a right . . . he passed under a flickering strip light and skirted around a janitor polishing the floor. Behind him, Mrs. Elwood was trotting furiously in an attempt to keep up.

"Are you sure this is the right way?" she panted. "We've gone awfully far."

"I'm sure," he said softly, without turning around.

"Of course. I'm sorry. But can we at least slow down a bit? My legs are a *teensy* bit shorter than yours."

For the first time that day, Jonathan smiled. "Yeah. We can do that."

There was a heavy door at the end of the hallway, and suddenly they were outside again. They had come out onto a small courtyard, where benches clustered around an ornate wooden shelter. Thick green plants were dotted around in ceramic pots. Jonathan guessed that visitors were supposed to relax out here, but you could never escape the fact that you were in a hospital. Orderlies wheeled gurneys back and forth, their wheels rattling on the uneven surface, and in front of him a pair of surgical gloves lay discarded on the ground.

In the corner of the courtyard there was a loading bay marked with yellow lines on the pavement, and beyond, hidden from sight of the courtyard, there was a small, grimy wing of the hospital. The crumbling Victorian brickwork was coated with soot and grime, and the rows of windows were all barred. Water dripped down from the gutters, forming a small pool near the doorway. It had been over a year since Jonathan had last visited the wing where his dad now lay.

Mrs. Elwood watched Jonathan thoughtfully. "I'd forgotten how ugly it was," she said.

"I wish I had."

"Do you want me to go first?"

He nodded.

She went over to the door and pushed it open. Inside they had made an effort to modernize the reception area: There were plastic chairs and watercoolers and a glass screen for the front desk. But a dingy atmosphere remained. Three people sat waiting, flicking silently through magazines. None of them looked up as Mrs. Elwood marched up to the reception desk and spoke to the nurse.

"Hello. We're here to see Alain Starling."

The nurse pursed her lips and consulted her clipboard. "Yes . . . I'm afraid we're not allowing any visitors into this wing at the moment. There have been some . . . disturbances."

"Are you sure? We've come a long way."

"I'm sorry. There's nothing I can do."

The nurse looked up, suddenly spotting Jonathan through the glass. "Oh, it's you."

"I want to see my dad," he said.

The nurse paused, weighing the situation. Eventually she relented. "You can go up, but only for ten minutes. He's in Room Seven."

The upstairs hallways were even colder and gloomier than the reception area. Jonathan passed through a large ward with a domed ceiling. The lights were on, but they were too weak to fill the entire room, and shadows bred in the corners and high up near the roof. Most of the patients lay in their beds, moaning quietly, but some wandered around in stained surgical gowns. A large man with a bristling, uncontrollable beard grabbed Jonathan's arm as he went by and hissed into his ear.

"He comes at night, you know. When no one can see him. When it's *dark*. Last night he took Griffin, but it could have been any of us. You have to help us!"

His eyes welled with tears, and there was a desperate edge to his voice. Jonathan carefully removed himself from his grasp and stepped away. "I'm sorry. I can't help you."

The man broke into sobs, and began beating himself

on the chest. A pair of orderlies ran past Jonathan and tried to restrain him. Jonathan ushered Mrs. Elwood away from the struggle and out of the ward. "Poor soul," she said. "It's dreadful when they lose their minds like that."

The patients were more vocal in the next ward, and the room rang with shouts and cries. Men stood talking to one another in guttural languages that Jonathan couldn't understand. One banged his fists loudly on the whitewashed walls, while another sat on the edge of his bed, rocking back and forth and muttering to himself. He looked up sharply as Jonathan walked by — his face was drenched with fear.

Jonathan was relieved when they emerged into a long, quiet corridor. The hospital staff had seen Alain enough times to take him straight to one of the private rooms on the very edge of the hospital. Room Seven was the penultimate room in the hallway. There was a pitiful whimpering noise coming from behind the next door, but Alain's room was silent. Jonathan took a deep breath and went inside.

Room Seven was a cramped space with only the bare minimum of furniture. Light was provided by a small lamp on the bedside table, and there was a musty smell in the air. Alain Starling was stretched out on the bed like a corpse. His skin was white and glistened with sweat. His face was contorted and his mouth wide open. There was a thin line of dribble running down his cheek. He didn't acknowledge his son.

"All right, Dad," said Jonathan cheerily. Truth be told, the sight of his dad after a darkening had stopped shocking him years ago. There had been a time, when he was younger, when he could barely look at Alain, but he had seen it too many times now.

"Hello, Alain," ventured Mrs. Elwood, a little more nervously.

"So how are you doing, Dad?" Jonathan dragged a chair to the bedside. "You don't look too bad. I've seen you worse." Alain Starling didn't move a muscle. Jonathan wiped the dribble away from his face with his sleeve. "That's a bit gross, though," he muttered.

"How are you feeling, Alain?" Mrs. Elwood asked.

No response. His eyes remained fixed on the ceiling. It was difficult to be certain that he was even breathing.

"D'you want to hear what's going on with me, then?" Jonathan tried. "Er . . . what've I been doing? Oh, I got suspended a few weeks ago. They caught me sitting around in Regent's Park when I should have been in school. Sorry about that. I was going to tell you but we hadn't been talking much and there didn't seem to be much point. They said if there was any more trouble they'd throw me out, but I don't think they will."

"Now, Jonathan," Mrs. Elwood said gently. "You know you shouldn't say those sorts of things. You'll only upset Alain."

Jonathan didn't respond. It was the most that he had said to his dad for maybe a year or more. At home the two of them generally kept out of each other's way, only occasionally bumping into each other in the kitchen or on the stairs. Jonathan believed that somewhere, deep down, his dad loved him, but he wasn't sure his father had the words to say it. Now, with Alain lying motionless next to him, it was easier to talk.

"So I thought I'd save them the trouble and drop out. Go traveling for a bit. See the world. I can get jobs abroad — you won't have to pay for anything. I think it'd be good for me. What do you think?"

He knew that his dad wasn't going to say anything, but he had to try. Jonathan and Mrs. Elwood took it in turns to talk to Alain, searching for something that might trigger a response. After several fruitless minutes the nurse tapped apologetically on the door. "I'm sorry, but you really have to leave now. The patients will be settling down soon."

They prepared to leave. When Jonathan was sure that Mrs. Elwood's back was turned, he briefly touched his dad on the arm, and then hurried out of the room.

As they made their way out of the hallway, a scream erupted from Room Eight.

"I can feel it!" a hollow voice wailed. "*He* is coming for me!"

Jonathan shivered, and headed down the stairs.

# 3

Outside, the weather was getting worse. A violent wind harassed Jonathan and Mrs. Elwood as they scurried across the hospital parking lot, and raindrops exploded on the pavement. It was a relief to get back into the car. They caught their breath in silence, the only sound was the water dripping from Jonathan's hair. Mrs. Elwood paused with her fingers on the car keys, the gloom unable to mask the pensive expression on her face.

Jonathan didn't know how the tiny woman had come to play such a large role in his life. There were countless mysteries and unanswered questions about his family, and Alain Starling declined to shed light on any of them. All Jonathan did know was that her constant, protective presence had been there for as long as he could remember.

When Jonathan had been given a small role in his elementary school play, it had been Mrs. Elwood who had sat in the audience and clapped at the end. She had been the one who had picked him up from the police station after he had been accused of shoplifting. And when Alain had been seriously ill a few years ago, it had been Mrs. Elwood who arrived unannounced in the kitchen, saying that she had bought a house down the street from the Starlings. She visited the house most days and was the closest thing to a mom that Jonathan had.

He had no idea what had happened to his real mom. Theresa Starling had disappeared before he was old enough to even remember her face. Alain protected the memory of his wife behind a shroud of silence, and refused to say a word on the subject. When Jonathan was ten, he had used a fishing trip to the local canal as an opportunity to ask his dad about Theresa. After thirty painful seconds Alain had marched off, leaving Jonathan alone with all the fishing gear. It was the angriest he had ever seen his dad. He didn't bother asking after that. His mom was gone and she wasn't coming back. All he was left with was her name.

"I know it's silly," cut in Mrs. Elwood, with a slight tremble in her voice. "I mean, I've seen him like that before, but . . . it still upsets me. I hope he won't be in the hospital too long this time."

"Yeah. Maybe."

Alain usually recovered in a few days, but there had been times when it had taken a lot longer. When Jonathan was ten his dad had lain frozen and silent for six months, and the doctors had told Mrs. Elwood that it was unlikely he was ever going to get better. In his darkest moments, Jonathan wondered whether it might have been for the best if he had not woken up a couple of mornings later. Most of the time it didn't seem like his dad wanted to be alive.

"You're going to stay with me while he recovers?"

Jonathan grimaced. "Do we have to have this argument again? You know I like to sleep in my own bed. I'll be fine in the house. It worked OK last time he was sick, didn't it?"

"I don't know. . . ." she said dubiously.

"You're only down the road. Come on — it's not like I see anything of Dad when he's well."

Mrs. Elwood sighed. "Yes, dear. I know that. Look, we'll see how things go tonight. Just make sure you keep your cell phone on. Any problems, give me a call. You promise?"

Jonathan made a mock Scout salute. "On my honor."

She started up the engine, and within an hour they were back outside Jonathan's house in a leafy area of North London. Its imposing walls stood firm against the onslaught of the rain, and the knotted undergrowth of the garden remained unmoved by the howling protest of the wind. Jonathan started to get out of the car, and then paused.

"Thanks," he said finally.

She smiled. "It's OK. It's not easy being you. I know that. But you're doing fine."

He gave her a humorless chuckle, and slammed the car door shut.

Jonathan had lived here for as long as he could remember. In a rare moment of openness, Alain had said they had lived somewhere else when Jonathan was a baby, some small, unnamed town up north. Where Alain had found the money to pay for this house was a mystery. There certainly wasn't much now; barely enough for food and school uniforms, let alone vacations and fixing up the house. Jonathan noted that the weeds were winning their battle with the driveway, and that the house was in desperate need of a coat of paint and some new gutters. He fumbled around in his pockets for the front door key, and entered his home.

It was only slightly warmer inside than it had been outside, but at least he was out of the rain. A draft came charging across the wooden floor to greet Jonathan, gnawing hungrily at his ankles. Shivering, he flicked on the hall switch, and a bulb flickered into life high up on the ceiling. In the gloom familiar things assumed ominous, alien shapes. Up the grand staircase, the pitch-black landing seemed to be hiding secrets and dangers. Jonathan felt a sudden urge to break the silence. "Hello?" he called out.

There was no response.

He shrugged. This was ridiculous. It was his house, after all. It wasn't as if he was a toddler. Jonathan had spent many nights alone, not knowing whether Alain was in the house, locked up in his study, or whether he had gone out somewhere. He hadn't gotten scared then — if anything, he had enjoyed the space. Most kids would love to have his freedom. Getting the creeps now seemed a bit pathetic.

He wandered into the kitchen, turning on lights as he went. It was nicer there, in the cleanest and most modern room in the house. The fridge hummed comfortingly. Jonathan poured himself a glass of orange juice and thought about making some food. He hadn't eaten since lunch, and it was getting late. On the other hand, he wasn't feeling very hungry and he couldn't be bothered to make himself anything complicated. He compromised on a bag of chips and an apple.

Outside, a black van rolled slowly up the street and came to a stop outside the Starling house. The driver switched off the headlights, but no one got out of the car.

Jonathan sat at the table and munched on his apple thoughtfully. Mrs. Elwood had promised to call the school tomorrow, so he was free until the weekend at least. No need to go to bed early tonight. He flipped through the TV guide, but there was nothing good on. For the hundredth time he cursed the fact that his dad had refused to pay for satellite television. Jonathan wasted a couple of weeks trying to persuade him, before concluding that Alain had no idea what it actually was.

There must be something he could do. Jonathan didn't mind spending time on his own — most of the time, he preferred it that way — but tonight he wanted to do more than lie on his bed and daydream. He didn't have a computer, though Mrs. Elwood had promised him that he was going to get a PlayStation for Christmas. Alain disapproved of computers. He told Jonathan that people should spend their time reading books instead. Nearly all of the rooms in the Starling house were crammed with books, mostly tattered old volumes with long titles, missing pages, and a strange musty odor to them. Alain was happiest when he was lost in a book, legs sprawled over the side of an armchair. Apparently he used to be an academic of some sort, though he didn't teach now. Instead he spent most of his days locked up in his study — and Jonathan had no idea what he did there. He had never been allowed in, and it was the only room in the house with a working lock on the door.

The wind had changed direction, sending the rain crashing against the kitchen window. Jonathan got up and pulled the blinds shut. As he did so, he thought he caught sight of something moving in the garden. It was difficult to be sure, among the tangle of the undergrowth. Probably just the cat from next door, Jonathan reassured himself. Nothing to be worried about. All the same, he double-checked that the back door was locked before he left the kitchen.

He decided to go to his room and watch TV in bed. Even if there was only some boring documentary on, or a house makeover show, it was better than moping around down here. He went through all the rooms on the first floor, drawing the curtains and checking that all the windows were closed. The weather was still filthy outside, but he couldn't see any more movement. When he thought everything was secure, Jonathan went up the stairs.

The landing was in a disheveled state. The rug covering the floorboards had been crumpled and one of the paintings had been knocked askew. Jonathan suddenly remembered that his dad had suffered a darkening here that day. The mess must have been caused by the paramedics as they tried to get him out. He straightened the painting and shook the rug flat, trying not to imagine the scene.

He was brushing his teeth when he heard a soft thud from somewhere near the back door. Whatever it was, it didn't sound like a cat. Outside the bathroom window, it was so dark it was hard to see, but he was convinced that there was *something* out there, a shape hunched by the side of the house. Had they tried to open the back door?

Jonathan reached for his cell phone and called Mrs. Elwood.

"Jonathan? Is everything all right?"

"I know it sounds stupid but . . . I think that there's someone prowling around outside. Should I call the police?"

"Not yet. It might be nothing. Stay where you are. I'll be over as soon as I can."

She hung up. Jonathan raced around the second floor, checking all the windows. Now every sound, every creak of the floorboards, and every splash of rain on the windows had a menacing tone to it. A click from downstairs stopped Jonathan in his tracks. It sounded like a door being quietly shut. The front door! He had forgotten to lock it! And now someone was in the house.

Jonathan's heart began to race wildly. He needed to find somewhere safe to hide until Mrs. Elwood got here. His first thought was to go somewhere in his bedroom, but hiding under the bed was for little kids. Instead,

Jonathan moved to the opposite end of the landing. He was wondering about trying to get onto the roof through his dad's bedroom window when he noticed that the door to the study was ajar. That must have been where Alain had experienced his darkening! For the first time in his life, Jonathan could enter the study.

He crept inside, closed the door, and carefully twisted the key in the lock until it clicked. There was definitely someone in the house. Though they were trying not to be heard, Jonathan could make out a careful tread of footsteps on the stairs. He sat on the floor with his back to the door and waited. It felt fairly sturdy, but would it be enough to keep out someone trying to get in? Around him everything was in darkness. Despite his situation, a voice in Jonathan's head whispered to him to turn on the lights and investigate the study. This might be his only chance.

The footsteps began to explore the second floor, spending a couple of minutes in Jonathan's room. Then there was silence. He pressed himself flat to the floor, and looked out through the crack underneath the door. First all he could see was the bathroom door, but then suddenly a pair of black shoes came into view. Jonathan lay very still, trying not to breathe, alarmed by the clamoring of his frantic heartbeat.

Above his head, the door handle began to turn slowly, until the lock stopped it. He hoped fervently that a locked door would put off the intruder, but the handle began to turn again, more forcefully this time. There was a high-pitched whining noise from the landing that sounded more animal than human. Jonathan froze as the door began to rattle violently. Abandoning all hope of hiding, he raced across the room to the desk and, straining with the pressure, pushed it across the door. On the landing the whining got louder, and there was an explosion of scratching on the door. The sound of the high-pitched scrabbling on the woodwork set his teeth on edge.

Jonathan began blindly piling objects on top of the desk: a chair, a heavy trash can, anything that could help to create a barrier. The intruder hammered on the door, which trembled under the force of the blows. Jonathan ran to the window and looked down at the ground, wondering if he could survive the jump to the garden. Then the banging and the scratching suddenly stopped. There was a pause. He held his breath in the silence.

"It's OK, Jonathan. It's me!"

It was Mrs. Elwood. He had never been so relieved to hear her voice. Jonathan pulled the objects away from the door and opened it. She was standing in her robe and slippers, with a golf club in her hands. Seeing the fear in his eyes, she started.

"My God! What's going on?"

"There was a burglar!" Jonathan gasped. "Someone broke in. . . ."

Mrs. Elwood gave him a dubious look. "I didn't see anyone. Are you sure your mind wasn't playing tricks on you?"

"Positive! There was someone here," Jonathan said desperately. "I'm not making it up! Look at the door!"

Mrs. Elwood peered up at the woodwork. The lacquered surface was crisscrossed with long white scratches. Her jaw hardened. "I see. Nasty. Come on. You can stay in my spare room tonight."

She took him gently by the arm, and Jonathan allowed himself to be led away, but not before he had locked the study door behind him. It might be a futile gesture, but it was the best he could do. For now, he had to leave the study and all its secrets intact.

# 4

Mrs. Elwood hummed cheerily as she bustled around the kitchen, stirring and flipping and buttering. She used a small stepladder to take things down from the high cupboards, scurrying up the steps with practiced ease. On the stove a pan of baked beans was bubbling away, and the air was heavy with the smell of fried bacon. In the background the radio was playing a pop song that had been a massive hit a few years ago. The morning had dawned bright and cold, and the room was filled with pale light.

At the kitchen table Jonathan blew on his cup of tea and took a cautious sip. It was hot and sweet — perfect. Lots of things seemed right about this morning, which made it all the more difficult not to feel a bit stupid about what had happened the night before. He felt less sure about what had been real and what hadn't. OK, *something* had happened to the study door, but had there really been an intruder? Mrs. Elwood hadn't seen anyone. Maybe it was just something to do with the wind. Maybe he had dreamed the whole thing up. Those terrified patients at the hospital must have gotten his imagination working overtime.

Mrs. Elwood brought over a plate of fried eggs and bacon and sat down opposite him. Jonathan didn't usually bother eating breakfast, but today he attacked the food voraciously.

"Careful. You'll give yourself indigestion."

Jonathan ignored her, and tore himself another mouthful of toast.

"So I called the school this morning and explained the situation to them. I have to say, they weren't very understanding. They asked a lot of questions, almost as if they didn't believe me. Do you know why that would be?"

He took a quick, guilty sip of tea. With his attendance record, he wasn't surprised no one believed her. "Dunno. Teachers are like that."

"Well, *eventually* they listened to me, and they said

that you don't need to worry about coming in for the rest of the week. What are you going to do with yourself? You can't sit with Alain all day long."

"Not sure yet. I want to go back to the house this morning. It's a bit of a mess, and I kind of want to clean it up. You know, if he gets better quickly and everything is in shambles . . ."

Mrs. Elwood nodded. She hadn't mentioned last night once, for which Jonathan was immensely grateful. "Of course. I've got to go into town later this morning, but I could come with you before then, if you want."

"Nah. I'll be all right."

She smiled, and left him alone to finish his breakfast.

At ten o'clock Jonathan made the short trip home. He hadn't been entirely honest with Mrs. Elwood. He did want to clean up the house, but the real prize was his dad's study. After all these years, this was his chance to really explore it. His heart rate pulsed faster just thinking about it. The house looked as decrepit as ever, but a little less foreboding than it had during the night. *There's no way that an intruder would dare to return here in daylight,* its windows seemed to wink at Jonathan; *burglars are cowards like that.* Still, he double-checked the road as he walked up the driveway. At this time of the morning, everything was quiet, and the only visible people were an elderly couple, presumably on their way to the shops, and a nanny pushing a baby along in a stroller.

Jonathan let himself in, and this time he made doubly sure the front door was locked behind him. He put one of his favorite CDs on in his bedroom to keep himself company and turned up the volume. Trying to keep calm, he busied himself with simple tasks: taking out the trash, doing the wash. Then, before he knew it, Jonathan was standing in front of the study, trying to ignore the raking scars that still marked the door. He took a deep breath, unlocked the door, and went inside.

It was dark in the study. The blinds had been pulled down over the window, so only the faintest chinks of light could shine through. There was a dank smell to the room, as if it hadn't been aired for years. Jonathan walked across the room, pulled up the blinds, and opened a window. Sunlight and biting fresh air streamed into the room. Immediately he felt better.

For all intents and purposes, the study had been Alain's world for the past few years. He worked here, ate his meals here, often fell asleep here. While Alain sat quietly, leafing through books, Jonathan would drift through the rest of the house like a ghost. If he wanted to speak to his dad, he had to knock three times on the door. If Alain had to leave the room he would swiftly lock it behind him, to prevent his son from catching a glimpse of what was going on inside. If Alain left the room of his own accord — to go to the bathroom or make himself a drink — and bumped into Jonathan, he would give him a brisk nod of recognition.

"Hello, son. Everything all right?"

"Fine."

"Good. Keep it up."

And with that, he would slip back inside and lock the door.

Jonathan had come to terms with his unusual family situation. He wasn't a great talker himself, and if there were any practical problems, there was always Mrs. Elwood. He would have been lying if he'd said that things were perfect, and that he didn't wish that his mother were still around, or that Alain were more of a normal dad. But that was just the way things were. He coped.

But now he was here, in his dad's private sanctum, and it was difficult to resist the urge to trash the room that had kept his dad away from him for so long. In actual fact, it was an unremarkable space. Bookshelves lined every wall and were stuffed with the sort of old, weighty books that had colonized the rest of the house. Yellowed newspaper clippings had been stuck on the walls, with lurid headlines that screamed TWO DIE IN COLLAPSED BUILDING HORROR, GRUESOME BLOOD-BANK ROBBERY, and LONDON WOLFMAN: AMAZING NEW SIGHTING! To Jonathan's left there was the heavy wooden desk that he had forced across the door last night. He tried to push it back to its original place, but without the panic and the adrenaline pumping through his veins he could barely move it an inch. In the chaos, pieces of paper had been scattered all over the floor, and there were pencils and pens everywhere. Whatever Jonathan had been expecting — some sort of crazy dungeon perhaps, with chains hanging from the wall and a rack in the center of the room — this certainly wasn't it.

As he looked around the shelves a framed photograph caught his eye. He lifted it up and inspected it.

It was a picture of a young couple, their arms wrapped around each other. They were standing in the rain in front of a grimy building with the sign BARTLEMAS TIMEPIECES daubed in white paint across it, but they were smiling and happy. Jonathan stared at it for a few seconds before realizing that the man in the photograph was Alain. Well, it wasn't the Alain that Jonathan knew. This man had blond hair, not gray, and he was standing upright, not hunched over. He didn't just look younger — he looked like a different person. Jonathan wondered what sort of man his father had been back then, whether he had fooled around and told jokes.

The woman he didn't recognize. She was young, with thick black hair that fell down to her shoulders. Two large, gold, hoop earrings poked out through the dark curls. She was wearing a strange gypsy outfit, with a white blouse and voluminous red patterned skirt. Must have been the fashion in those days, he guessed. There was a sense of mischief in her smile, and her eyes were gray and defiant.

Gray eyes. With a jolt Jonathan realized that he was looking at a picture of his mother. He had never seen a picture of her before. Alain had always said that there weren't any. He had been lying all this time. At once all the resentment, the bitter anger that Jonathan had spent so many years keeping trampled down, rose to the surface. He threw the photo against the wall, and sank to his knees as the frame shattered. For the first time in his life, he began to cry.

Feeling a bit embarrassed, Jonathan blew his nose on a ragged tissue and tried to pull himself together. This wasn't achieving anything, although, in a strange way, he felt better for having cried. He went over to the photograph. The frame was ruined but the photograph was untouched. Carefully, he extracted it from the frame and placed it on the writing desk.

Why had his dad lied to him? Jonathan could understand why Alain had not wanted to talk about his wife's disappearance, but lying about a photograph? It didn't make any sense. It just seemed pointlessly cruel. He looked around at the books and the scraps of paper. Maybe the answer lay in here somewhere. At random Jonathan picked up a book and began to read.

Two long hours later he had learned nothing. There didn't seem to be any common theme to the books in

Alain's study. It was as if he'd gathered a hundred random volumes and put them on his shelves. Old history books, political textbooks, poetry books, and even a selection of personal diaries. The only thing they had in common was the fact that they were deathly boring. In some of them Alain had placed bookmarks at certain pages, and circled or underlined specific passages. For example, in *Eminence: My Life with Professor Carl von Hagen*, a diary by a serving maid called Lily Lamont, the following section had been highlighted:

*19th October, 1925: After the hubbub and excitement of the past few days, my master was quiet today. He spent the day locked up in his laboratory, refusing all my offers of food and drink. Towards the evening he appeared, with a wild and ferocious look in his eyes. He mentioned something about the "darkest side" underneath his breath, before picking up his hat and greatcoat and stepping out into the night. I was not to see him for several days afterwards.*

Which was slightly more interesting, but Jonathan didn't have the foggiest idea what it meant. Nor could he decipher the importance of a slender book called *The Criminal Underbelly of Victorian Britain*, which was crammed with bookmarks. According to the date on its inside cover, it was written by a man called Jacob Entwistle way back in 1891, making him wonder what the point was in reading it. Nevertheless, on page seventy-nine Alain had marked the following passage:

*In the foul depths of Pentonville Gaol I came across a particularly wretched specimen called Robert Torbury, a pickpocket and petty thief. He had been languishing behind bars for many years, and his mind had wasted away as a consequence. When he laid his eyes upon me he grabbed at my clothing, imploring me to help him. He was being sent away, he gabbled nonsensically at me, he had been sentenced to live in the darkness. As he sobbed I wondered what sane man could listen to him and still maintain that the legal system of the British Empire remains the fairest in the civilized world. . . .*

Jonathan closed the book with a thump, raising a cloud of dust. This was getting him nowhere. He turned his attention to the scraps of paper on the floor. They were covered in the scrambled thoughts that Alain had managed to scribble down. Luckily most of them were dated, so in about ten minutes Jonathan was able to put them in some sort of chronological order. The most recent entry had been made the day before his dad had suffered a darkening. It read simply: "A crossing? Surely I must be close now."

Beneath it there was the name of a book — *The Darkest Descent* — and a page number, with a code after it that he realized was a library reference number. Jonathan felt a little tremor of excitement. Could this book have something to do with whatever dark secret had been haunting Alain for all these years? He couldn't be sure, but he knew one thing — he had to get his hands on that book. And there was only one place in London where he would be able to find it.

# 5

The car of the Northern Line tube train rattled furiously as it made its hidden progress underneath the streets and houses of London. Above the surface it was fresh and overcast, but down in the tunnels the air was stiflingly hot and the harsh lighting hurt Jonathan's eyes. Although it was midmorning, and all the commuters had long since reached their offices, the tube car was still jammed with people, and his face was at an uncomfortable proximity to an overweight tourist's armpit. Jonathan glanced up at the Underground map on the wall of the car, to count how many stops he had to go until he could escape the arid prison.

The piece of paper he had taken from Alain's study was folded safely into his jeans' pocket. From time to time he slipped his fingers into the pocket to reassure himself that it was still there. The instant he had read it he had realized where he had to go. Jonathan knew his father well enough to know that he would not be able to pick up *The Darkest Descent* at his local library. It would not be sitting alongside cheap murder mysteries and romance novels. More than likely, Alain had been the only person who had ever wanted to read the book. No, there was only one place where he would be able to discover its secrets: the British Library.

If there was one aspect of life that Alain had tried to teach his son about, it was reading. Jonathan had many early memories of sitting in his dad's lap with a big book on his knees, spelling out words and laughing at the funny pictures. Alain seemed more at ease dealing with unreal worlds and fantasy stories than real life. He took Jonathan on regular visits to libraries across London, and made sure that he was a registered patron at all of them. They would sit side by side at one of the long reading desks, Jonathan copying the careful way in which his dad turned the pages. In all those years it was the closest they ever got to each other.

The tube came to a sudden, jarring halt as it pulled into King's Cross Station. Those who disembarked were herded like livestock toward three turnstiles, not nearly enough for the amount of people trying to get through. With a great amount of pushing and swearing, the crowd fought to be at the front of the swell. Jonathan waited at the back, brimming with impatience. With his dad in the hospital, it was up to him to continue Alain's desperate quest, even though Jonathan wasn't sure what he was looking for or what secrets awaited him in the pages of *The Darkest Descent*. All he did know was that he was close, and that he was determined to find some answers.

With its complex series of twisting tunnels and staircases, King's Cross Underground resembled a living organism. Humans flowed through its veins and arteries like red blood cells, racing and colliding against one another. Whichever platform they were heading for, whether it was for the Victoria Line, the Metropolitan Line, or the Piccadilly Line, they all seemed to know exactly where they were going, always kept their gaze fixed directly in front of them. Jonathan cut into the slipstream of people and circled up and out of the station.

It felt good to be outside, despite the fact that it had started to spit with rain. In front of the station there was some major sort of construction work going on, and parts of the road had been dug up. The sound of drilling rang in Jonathan's ears. With all the barriers and contradictory pedestrian signs it wasn't obvious which was the way to the library, but Jonathan knew the route. He went right past St. Pancras Station, King's Cross's gloomy older brother, narrowly avoided getting knocked down crossing Midland Road, and found himself at his destination.

The British Library was a modern, redbrick building on a corner of Euston Road. Jonathan wandered past a coffee shop and entered the front yard. Around him there were raised, neatly clipped hedges and large rocks balanced at even intervals on plinths. There was an overwhelming atmosphere of order and calm about the layout. To his left, a big bronze statue of a crouching man peeped over the hedges at Jonathan. Behind the library's gently sloping roof, the gothic tower of St. Pancras Station loomed over it, trapped in a cage of scaffolding.

Jonathan trudged through the yard and through the automatic doors that marked the entrance to the library.

Inside it was bright and spacious. He was in the foyer area of a vast main hall. In front of him a network of floors and staircases rose up to the roof, like the cross section of an ants' nest. To his left, a large painting slashed with vivid colors stretched across the wall. Somewhere in the hall, a recording of African tribal music was playing, and the noise of the drums drowned out the chattering of the people around him. If anything, the scene resembled a posh department store more than a library.

Jonathan went straight up the narrow escalator to the first floor, and then wandered past a giant glass bookcase filled with old books that made him think of home. The reading room was tucked away in the left-hand corner of the first floor. The librarian at the front desk smiled in recognition when she saw him.

"Hello, Jonathan. Where's your dad?"

"Hi, Jenny. He's sick again. But there's this book that I *really* need to read for school, and I can't find it anywhere else."

"You know you're too young to come in on your own."

"Come on, Jenny. I'm always here. And it's only one book!"

The librarian frowned, and then leaned forward and said in a whisper, "OK. This once. But I'm going to get in terrible trouble if anything goes wrong."

Jonathan grinned. "It's a library! What can go wrong?"

He moved on past the desk, and found himself a seat in a secluded corner of the reading room. There was something very particular about the place — the low ceiling, the muted lighting, the smell of the carpet — that brought back memories of the time Jonathan had spent here in silent admiration watching his dad read. Within these walls it had almost been possible to pretend that they had a normal father–son relationship. He shook his head. There was no time for that sort of thing now.

Getting books from this library wasn't as simple as pulling them off the shelves. Jonathan had to type the name of the book he wanted and his seat number into one of the banks of computers installed near the reading desks. Then the librarians would bring it up from storage. Jonathan liked to imagine that, deep in underground London, there was a vast labyrinth of books, cavern after cavern, which librarians searched with powerful flashlights and weapons. When his book had been retrieved, a light would flick on at his reading desk. There was no way of knowing how long that would be. Until then, he would just have to wait. Jonathan sat back in his chair and felt himself dozing off.

He awoke with a start. Since he had fallen asleep the reading room had filled up, and every available space around him had been taken. He hoped that he hadn't been snoring. The light on his desk was on, and Jonathan went up to the main desk to collect the book. The elderly librarian looked up sharply when he heard Jonathan's request and placed a black, unassuming volume on the counter. Then he opened a register and handed Jonathan a pen.

"You'll have to sign here."

"I've never had to do this before."

The librarian said nothing, merely tapped the page with his pen. Only three signatures had been entered into the register, the earliest entry a Horace Carmichael back in 1942. Jonathan added his name to the list and headed back to his seat. The librarian silently watched him go.

Now that it was in his hands, Jonathan felt the excitement building within him. Resisting the urge to go straight to the page number his dad had written down, he leafed through the book's pages. According to the introduction, *The Darkest Descent* had been written by a man called Raphael Stevenson, who in Victorian times had been a famous explorer. He had spent the early parts of his life traveling around distant corners of the earth, meeting foreign tribes and fighting off wild animals. However, in his mid-forties Stevenson had gone insane, and he had been committed to an asylum. The page that Alain had referenced came toward the end of the book, where the writing started to become strange and evasive:

*On returning from my travels in the Indian subcontinent, I succumbed to a dull lethargy that left me lying dazed and listless in my bed for days on end. At first I believed that I had caught some kind of foreign virus, but then I realized that, instead, my life was merely lacking the day-to-day excitements and dangers that I had experienced abroad. One foggy evening I resolved to raise myself from my slumber and spend my nights in search of . . . darkness.*

*My nighttime wanderings took me deeper into the black heart of London, where women stood cackling like fowl outside public houses and men hid in doorways with evil intent. More than once I owed a debt of gratitude to my stout walking stick. However, after a period of time I became more accustomed to the nefarious character of the area and felt able to speak to its denizens.*

*At first my clothing and demeanor attracted suspicion, but gradually people began to open up to me. I spent shilling after shilling buying drinks in dirty gin palaces, trying to extract information from the lowest and most shameful creatures in London. But whenever I would bring up the subject of darkness and its whereabouts, they would share a meaningful glance and fall silent. Sometimes one of them would start to speak, only to be quieted by the others. The more people I talked to, the more I became convinced that there was some sort of evil wasteland here in our very capital, the glittering cornerstone of the British Empire.*

*My ceaseless probings were yielding no results, and I was on the verge of ending my quest, when I met a young street urchin called Molly in a seedy part of*

Clerkenwell. She responded positively to my gentle words, and promised to show me the way to an area of London she swore I could never before have witnessed.

Our journey was a haphazard one, taking account of all manner of loops and changes of direction. When I questioned her about it she looked up with serious eyes and told me that we were following the path of the River Fleet. The River Fleet! A foul and noxious tributary that had been bricked over decades beforehand, such was the unsavory character of its grim waters. I asked Molly how she could still follow its course, and she replied, "I can feel it rushing through my veins."

As we walked briskly down to the River Thames, her mood suddenly changed, and she became very agitated, begging me to turn back and go home. I remained resolute, and we came out under the shadow of Blackfriars Bridge, where the Fleet flowed into the Thames. The river was at low tide, and we climbed down to the riverbed, where Molly showed me the *yawning gateway to darkness. She fell to her knees sobbing, pleading with me not to pass through it, but my mind was made up. Had I known what I know now, I would have listened to her. . . .*

Jonathan clenched his fist. This was what Alain had been looking for! And now he had found it too. He scribbled the details down onto a piece of paper.

At the desk next to him, a woman sighed loudly as she turned over the page of her book. She was dressed in an all-white pantsuit, with her hair dyed a vibrant purple. When Jonathan turned to look at her, she caught his eye and smiled. He stared back, entranced by the white pallor of her skin. Her smile broadened, and she looked conspiratorially left and right before leaning forward and offering her hand. There was something very familiar about her, but the scent of her perfume haunted Jonathan's nostrils, disrupting his train of thought.

"I'm Marianne," she whispered. "My book is very boring."

"Um, I'm Jonathan," he replied. There was a pause. She appeared to be waiting for him to say something. "Why don't you read something else, then?"

"Nice to meet you, Jonathan. I would take out another book, but it takes so long to order one, and I have to go soon. Is your book interesting?"

He shrugged.

"Can I have a look at it?"

It was getting darker outside, and the rain was now beating out a thunderous rhythm on the window. There was an alarm bell ringing at the back of Jonathan's mind, telling him to be careful. He wasn't sure that giving the woman his book was necessarily a good idea, but for some reason he was desperate not to disappoint her.

"Be careful. It's very old."

She took the book from his hands, frowning at the weight of it. "And heavy." She sniffed the front cover. "Smelly too."

Jonathan giggled. He really wasn't feeling like himself. Maybe it was something to do with her perfume, which had a very sweet odor to it. In the next seat, Marianne carefully read the title of the book out loud.

"*The Darkest Descent*. I think your book definitely *is* more interesting than mine. What a funny title. Why did you get this one out?"

Jonathan had to stop himself from blurting the answer out loud. "I . . . my teacher told us to read it. It's part of our history coursework."

She narrowed her eyes playfully. "Jonathan, you're not lying to me, are you? That's very rude, especially to a stranger. You should never lie to strangers, you know."

He shrugged again. Maybe it was time to get out of here. She had caught sight of the note he had made and was staring intently at it.

"What have you written down there? Something else for your 'teacher,' no doubt. Why don't you let Marianne have a little peek at it?"

"I have to go."

Jonathan tried to rise, but Marianne grabbed his wrist. He was surprised by how firm her grip was. He would have shouted out, but she was murmuring calming words under her breath, and he didn't feel *that* scared, not really, and he might as well sit down next to the pretty lady with the purple hair for a little while longer.

"That's better, isn't it?" she cooed in his ear. "Now, let's have a look at that note."

Jonathan looked on dreamily as she reached across and unfurled the scrap of paper. "A crossing point? You really have been naughty, lying to me. You've been reading about Darkside, haven't you? Tell Marianne what you know about Darkside, little one."

He giggled again, his head swimming. "It's some kind of weird place or something," he said. "Dunno really."

Marianne clapped her hands together in delight. "Well, you're going to find out! You're going to Darkside, Jonathan! And believe me, you'll have much more fun going with us than on your own. It can be a bit danger-ous there sometimes. It's good to have company."

Jonathan allowed himself to be pulled up out of his seat and led out of the reading room. Marianne was hold-ing his hand tightly, and walking briskly toward the stairs leading down to the main entrance.

"Where we going?" he slurred.

"Shhh . . . We're going to meet my friends Humble and Skeet, and then we're going for a little drive. You see?"

There were two men standing in the foyer at the front of the hall, one much taller and more still than the other. Marianne gave them both an enthusiastic wave. The smaller man jumped around in response.

The last remaining spark of Jonathan's consciousness was urging him to run, but his legs were betraying him, and he felt powerless to move away from Marianne. They took slow, deliberate steps down the staircase, and Jonathan realized that the woman was worried he was going to fall over. He tried to concentrate on keeping his footing. After all, he didn't want to let her down. . . .

A man walking in the opposite direction stumbled on the step, knocking into Marianne. She cursed, losing her grip on Jonathan's arm. Suddenly the link between them had been broken, and he could feel his head clearing a little. He was in danger — he had to move. Jonathan pelted away up the staircase, beyond Marianne's despairing lunge, skidded around a corner, and disappeared from view.

He had no idea where he was going. All he knew was that he had to get as much distance between himself and that strange woman as possible. Jonathan flew past the coffee shop on the first floor, ignoring the stares of the people sitting there. He headed up another staircase, taking two steps at a time. From somewhere there was a shout, whether from a librarian or Marianne he wasn't sure. He didn't look behind him to check.

His head felt better now. It felt like Marianne had put some sort of spell on him, but Jonathan knew that wasn't possible. One thing was definite, though: She had mentioned a place called Darkside. His dad had been onto something, and now Jonathan could pick up the trail.

He ran up the staircase until it came out onto the top floor. Though the bustle and chatter from the main hall carried up here, there was no one to be seen. Slowing down to a walk, Jonathan went over to the front edge of the walkway and looked down. From up here, everything in the main hall seemed normal. Knots of schoolchildren and students talked and laughed together, while others sat in the comfy seats scribbling on notepads or typing on laptops. Jonathan strained to catch a glimpse of Marianne. She was standing casually by the entrance, playing absentmindedly with a strand of her hair. The two men were nowhere to be seen. Suddenly she looked up in Jonathan's direction, and he pulled away from the ledge.

There was no guarantee that he was still safe. For all he knew, the two goons could be heading up toward him. And there was only one exit from the library that he knew about, and currently Marianne was standing right in front of it. Jonathan supposed that he could ask one of the librarians for help, but he didn't think his chances of explaining his problem were so good. Adults tended not to trust him, and he doubted that the kidnapping story would be swallowed that easily: *"You see, there's this woman who puts some kind of spell on you. . . ."* No, that wasn't going to work. There didn't even seem to be a fire alarm he could pull.

At the far corner of the walkway, Jonathan caught sight of the smaller henchman reaching the top floor. He sniffed the air eagerly with his long nose, his jittery movements turning in Jonathan's direction. Well, that settled it. He was going to have to do something. Moving quickly again, Jonathan rushed past the bathrooms and toward the bright shelter of a reading room, with the inscription MAPS lit up above the doorway. As he moved forward, the other henchman reached the top of the staircase on Jonathan's side in a calm, regular stride.

By the side of the entrance, a sign informed readers that neither pencils nor bags were allowed in the map room. A hint of a smile appeared on Jonathan's lips.

*    *    *

In the foyer, Marianne anxiously scanned the top floor for any sight of a commotion. It had looked like things were going as smoothly as they had in Trafalgar Square . . . and then that *fool* had knocked into her. She swore under her breath. Now she had to trust that Humble and Skeet could flush the boy out without alerting the authorities. It was a miracle that they hadn't been noticed yet. Marianne knew that her special perfume could deflect attention for a certain amount of time, but not with all this running around. Even now, she noticed a frown on the face of one of the library staff, as if he was trying to remember something he had forgotten.

Then she saw Jonathan moving down the escalator, with a librarian holding him firmly by the arm. He was grinning triumphantly. Humble and Skeet followed several paces behind him, helpless onlookers. At the sight of this procession a security guard moved toward them, but the librarian shook her head.

"I don't think that'll be necessary," she said wearily.

"All this because of a pencil?" Jonathan protested. "I can't believe you're throwing me out just because I was carrying a stupid pencil!"

"You were threatening to color in the maps," the librarian replied. "Priceless antique maps. That's why we're throwing you out. We'll have to confiscate your library card as well."

Jonathan gave an exaggerated sigh, then handed over the card. He nodded briskly at Marianne, headed out through the doors, then sprinted off at a breakneck pace. The librarian turned to Marianne. "Kids. I don't know what parents these days are thinking of, bringing them up to be like that."

Marianne nodded sympathetically. The librarian sighed again, and then began trudging back to the map room. As soon as she was out of sight, the shorter man came buzzing up to Marianne.

"You want Skeet to follow the puppy?"

"No need." Marianne looked out at the glowering sky. "We know where he's going already."

# 6

Jonathan didn't stop running until he had made it back to King's Cross. This time he dove gratefully into the hordes of people waiting on the platform; trying to find him now would be like looking for a needle in a haystack. He only had to wait for a minute or so until a train stuttered into the station and he squeezed aboard, all the while keeping an eye out for any pursuers. As the doors beeped closed, Jonathan felt a sigh of relief. He had escaped.

After a couple of stops the tube car started to empty. Jonathan took a seat and thought furiously. He knew that he was going to hunt for the crossing point described in Stevenson's journal, but he couldn't just disappear without telling anyone. However, if the kidnappers at the library were related to the intruder at the house, then it wasn't safe to go home. They could be there already. He could go to Mrs. Elwood's, but Jonathan doubted she would be home until later, and he didn't feel like hiding out in her garden until she returned. The perfect solution would have been to go over to a friend's place, but he didn't have any friends.

No, there was only one place he could go. Jonathan hopped off the tube two stops before the one nearest his house and walked briskly to the bus stop on the main road. From here he knew he could catch a ride up to the hospital.

When it eventually appeared, the bus followed a long, winding route that seemed to take in every backstreet in London. The streetlights were flickering on in the residential areas, and as he gazed out of the window Jonathan saw parents returning home from work, carefully pulling their cars into driveways and shutting the front door on the outside world. Beside him an old woman was jabbering away to herself and smelling as though she hadn't washed for a long time. The panic and the elation Jonathan had experienced in the library was ebbing away, only to be replaced by a simmering resentment. In the space of a day he had uncovered more about his family than his dad had told him during his entire lifetime. Why had Alain not told him about Darkside? What was so important that he couldn't tell his own son? What else was he hiding?

St. Christopher's Hospital was wreathed in darkness by the time he arrived. The wind lashed across Alain's wing, rattling the grimy windows and making the rotten door frames creak in agony. It seemed to Jonathan that, at any moment, the entire building could be torn from its foundations and carried away on the gale, taking its occupants with it. A sense of urgency descended upon him.

Inside, the reception area was deserted, except for a man in a robe who was staring intently at the ground, muttering something under his breath. Eventually the nurse appeared from one of the side rooms. She recognized Jonathan, and sent him crisply up to the first floor.

"The patients are a bit on edge tonight," she warned. "Keep your eyes down and don't hang around in the wards."

Jonathan moved quickly up the steps and into the first ward. The panicky racket of yesterday was gone, and an atmosphere of subdued agitation hung heavy in the air. Patients huddled in their beds, mewling softly with fear. He could even hear the occasional choked sob. A host of orderlies prowled watchfully around the room. Jonathan kept moving, following the nurse's instruction. Something was terribly wrong in this place.

Inside Room Seven, Mrs. Elwood was sitting next to the prostrate body of his dad, reading a glossy celebrity magazine. She whirled around at Jonathan's entrance, but Alain didn't move a muscle.

"Jonathan! What are you doing here? If you wanted to come you should have phoned me, dear. I would have picked you up."

He ignored her and strode up to Alain's bed. "What's Darkside, Dad?"

Behind him Mrs. Elwood whispered a quick prayer. He might have been imagining it, but Jonathan thought that one of his dad's eyes had twitched in recognition at the name.

"I've been in your study, Dad. Can you hear me? I've been in your precious study." He said it forcefully, like a challenge. Alain's lips trembled. He could hear what Jonathan was saying, all right. "I've been reading your stupid books."

Mrs. Elwood laid a restraining hand on his arm, but he shook her off. He was filled with a sudden anger that was clawing at his insides. A low moan escaped from Alain's lips, like the sound of some ancient Egyptian tomb opening.

"I saw the photograph, Dad. I saw the photograph of you and Mom."

Another moan, louder this time.

"All these years, and you never showed me. You told me there weren't any pictures!"

Nearly weeping with frustration, Jonathan turned away and sat on the end of his dad's bed. He wanted to hurt him, to pay him back for all those years of silence, to make him angry, to make him get up off his bed and fight back, anything. He needed Alain to be alive here with him. Shaking with rage, Jonathan felt like screaming at the top of his lungs to block everything else out, but then suddenly the anger was melting away and his dad was hugging him for the first time in years.

"I'm . . . so . . . sorry," he breathed in Jonathan's ear.

"It's all right," Jonathan managed to say back, his eyes tightly closed. "It's all right, Dad."

It was incredibly frustrating. Thinking that he might get some real answers this time, Jonathan asked his dad question after question. But Alain drifted in and out of consciousness, only catching snatches of what his son was saying. Sometimes he tried to reply, but his mouth struggled to form the words. Jonathan hung his head disconsolately.

"Don't worry, dear." Mrs. Elwood smiled sympathetically. "He's woken up. That's the main thing. When he's better you can ask him all the questions you want."

"It's just that there's so much I don't know. So much he hasn't told me." A thought occurred to him. "What do you know about Darkside?"

Mrs. Elwood sighed. As she turned her head away slightly, the lamp cast a shadow on her cheek. "Enough to know it's an evil place and that both you and your father would do well to stay away from it."

From the hallway outside there came the sound of measured footsteps. For a second Jonathan thought it was a nurse coming to tell them that they had to leave, but the footsteps passed by the door and went into Room Eight instead.

"But I know how to get there! I went to the British Library and read this book and it told me everything I need to know! I can go to Darkside!"

Roused, she pointed at Alain. "Do you really think it's that simple? Going to Darkside isn't like walking down a street, Jonathan. You can't just hop on a bus. It tears away pieces of your soul. Look at your dad! He hasn't been back there for twelve years, and that place still claws at his insides." She grabbed Jonathan's shoulders, her eyes wide and imploring. "It's like an addiction. Do you want to end up like that?"

"I don't understand. If he wants to go back so much, why doesn't he?"

Mrs. Elwood sighed. "There was an accident. A building collapsed on top of the only crossing point that Alain knew. He couldn't use it again. Ever since then, he's been obsessed with trying to find another way to get to Darkside. Lord knows he's got reason to go there, but . . . I mean, what *is* it about your family — why are you so willing to hurt yourselves?"

A scrabbling noise and a high-pitched whine carried through the wall from the room next door, distracting Jonathan. He forced himself to focus on Mrs. Elwood. "Look, someone's going to have to start telling me the truth. What is Darkside? What's my dad got to do with it? And why are some people trying to kidnap me?"

She blinked. "What?"

"They came for me in the library! There was this strange woman called Marianne, and she had this perfume that made me feel drowsy, and I was walking out with her until I managed to get away and I had to get thrown out to escape them."

There was a shocked pause.

"You were thrown out of the British Library?"

"I didn't have any choice! These guys were after me. I had to get out somehow!"

His explanation didn't appear to make things any better. "*And* I'm pretty sure that they were the same people who broke into the house last night."

Alain stirred, gazing inquiringly at Mrs. Elwood. All of a sudden she looked flustered. "I was going to tell you, Alain — but I wasn't sure how to put it. . . . Anyway, you've only just woken up and . . . look, there was a disturbance at your house last night. I got there in time and everything was fine but . . . I think something might have been after Jonathan. Obviously there's been some strange things going on, Alain, but we'll be just fine until you're well again. I can take care of Jonathan, ladies with strange perfume or not."

With a superhuman effort Alain stretched out a thin hand and rubbed Mrs. Elwood's arm comfortingly. Then, very slowly, he shook his head. "'Arn 'Eegi," he mumbled at his two visitors.

"What, Dad?"

"'Arn 'Eegi," he tried again, visibly frustrated with his mouth's inability to form words.

"I don't get it. What?"

Alain raised his head from the pillow and shouted, "'Arn 'EEGI!"

Mrs. Elwood gasped. "Surely not, Alain. We can take care of things here ourselves. We don't need to involve *him* . . . and you know what it means, don't you? You know where Jonathan will have to go!"

"What's he talking about?"

Alain's head slumped back onto the pillow. "S'only way," he slurred. "He knows . . . he can crossh." A faint smile flickered across his face.

"What's he saying? I don't get it. Please tell me."

Mrs. Elwood turned her head away again. "He's saying 'Carnegie.' He wants Carnegie to look after you."

"And who's Carnegie?"

"A friend of your father's. He lives in Darkside." She

was interrupted by a series of crashes from Room Eight, followed by a high-pitched scream that was drenched with fear. "What in God's name was that?"

There was another scream and the sound of breaking glass.

"I dunno. Doesn't sound good, though."

They heard the door in the next room being thrown open, and the sound of quick footsteps echoing down the corridor. Jonathan got up and cautiously peered around the door. In the gloom he could just about make out a figure hurrying away to the stairs.

"Jonathan, I'm sure the doctors know what they're doing."

"I don't think that was a doctor."

"Well, don't go out there. Jonathan!"

It was too late. He slipped out into the hall. There was a frosty breeze coming from somewhere and the door to Room Eight was banging frantically against the wall. Jonathan inched toward it and, taking a deep breath, looked into the room.

There had been an almighty struggle. The bed had been overturned and the sheets were strewn all over the floor. The lamp had been smashed and there were splatters of blood on the walls. Something had been thrown out of the window with tremendous force, smashing through the glass and the security bars beyond them. There was no one in the room. Both the visitor and the patient had gone. But Jonathan had only seen one person walking away down the hall. He went slowly over to the window and peered through. Far down below there was a body lying spread-eagled out on the pavement, resting on a bed of glass fragments. As he watched, another figure came out of the ward's main door, moved quickly past the body without a glance, and disappeared into the night.

Jonathan made to return to his father's room, but as he was leaving, something caught his eye on the floor. He bent down and picked it up. It was a slender silver knife with a handle that looked as if it had been carved from bone. The blood-smeared blade glinted with intent. With strange certainty, Jonathan knew that this wasn't the first time it had bitten into human flesh.

He could hear people on the stairs, probably coming to see what all the noise was about. Jonathan was aware he should drop the dagger, but for some reason he didn't move. There was something reassuring about the weight of the weapon in his hand; it seemed to fit snugly in his grasp. It felt almost as if the knife had been made for him. Deadly as it was, it also had an eerie beauty and, suddenly, he couldn't bear to let go.

There was no more time to think. Jonathan hurriedly wiped the blade clean, placed it in his pocket, and slipped back inside his dad's room.

"What's going on in there?" asked Mrs. Elwood.

He saw the concerned look on her face, and then shrugged. "Not sure," he lied.

A cry of pain from the bed made them both turn around. Alain had sat bolt upright in bed, hands clenched into fists, his whole body racked with spasms.

"My God. What's wrong?"

Veins were bulging in Alain's neck and his eyes were wild, as if he was trying to scream out one final warning, but all that escaped through his gritted teeth was a piercing, choking sound. Jonathan raced toward him but there was nothing he could do; Alain screamed and fell back onto the bed, eyes gazing blankly at the ceiling. The darkness had reclaimed him once more.

# 7

They stopped back at the Starling house only long enough to stuff some clothes into a backpack and wolf down some food. Mrs. Elwood was insistent that Jonathan reach the crossing point as soon as he could. "If you're going to cross you should do it now, before it gets too late." She gave a worried glance at the night sky. "We don't want anyone coming for you tonight."

As they were leaving the house, she scribbled down Carnegie's address on a piece of paper and handed it to Jonathan. Then she took a small object from her handbag, toying with it in her hands for a second. "There's a chance that you might need this," she said eventually. "Carnegie's a good friend of Alain's but he can be . . . awkward sometimes. If you're having any problems with him, then show him this. It should make things easier."

He peered closely at the object in her palm. It was a small, misshapen lump of metal. "What is it?"

"It *was* a bullet."

Jonathan gave Mrs. Elwood a suspicious look. "So if I have any trouble with this guy, I show him a used bullet?"

"That's right, yes."

"Couldn't I have a new bullet instead? And a gun?"

Mrs. Elwood reached up and gave him a fierce hug.

They drove through London in silence, lost in their own thoughts. The radio news was reporting on the disappearance of Ricky Thomas. The police still had no leads. Now that he had time to think about things, Jonathan could feel the apprehension rising within him. From what he had read and heard about the place, it didn't sound like Darkside was the safest place in the world. And now he had to travel there on his own, with a gang of kidnappers on his trail. He hoped that Carnegie *was* a good friend, because he needed one more than ever right now.

They had to halt driving west on Upper Thames

Street. There must have been some sort of accident up ahead, because both sides of the road were jammed solid with cars. Jonathan was on the verge of telling Mrs. Elwood that maybe they should go to the police instead of continuing the journey when he spotted a tall, familiar figure in a black suit walking slowly along the pavement toward them.

"Oh God," he whispered.

Mrs. Elwood turned around. "What is it?"

"It's him. Humble! One of the guys at the library I was telling you about. He's walking toward us now. Look!"

He was about eight car lengths away, moving as solemnly as if he were carrying a coffin. Though he wasn't closing in quickly, he was still closing in.

"How did they know I was here? Can't we drive away somewhere?" Jonathan asked, his stomach lurching with panic.

Mrs. Elwood threw her hands up in despair. "The road's blocked solid. There's nowhere to go. Anyway, he wouldn't dare do anything in public. We're surrounded by people, Jonathan."

The tall figure was starting to fill up the rearview mirror. He had to be seven feet tall at least.

"I was surrounded by people in the British Library, and they got me there too! We're not safe, I'm telling you!"

The giant was close enough now for the smile on his face to be visible. It looked as if he were welcoming an old friend. Mrs. Elwood began to look less certain.

"Are all the doors locked?"

"Yes, but . . . "

It was too late now: He was alongside the car. For a second Jonathan thought the giant was going to keep on walking, but at the last moment he stopped. He bent stiffly down to Jonathan's window and gave him a mute wave, a grin still plastered over his face.

"Don't look at him!" Mrs. Elwood began futilely beeping her horn. "Why can't we move?"

Jonathan couldn't have looked away if he tried. He was transfixed. The giant knocked on the window with surprising gentleness. It was all Jonathan could do to shake his head. The giant shrugged, and wrapped his huge fingers around the door handle.

"What is he doing?" Mrs. Elwood gasped.

Humble braced himself and began to pull. Unbelievably, the metal door began to creak and buckle.

"Oh my God!" Mrs. Elwood screamed. "He's ripping the door off!"

It seemed impossible, but he was. A sliver of light appeared between the door and the car, and it was starting to widen. Around them, the other drivers kept on chatting with their passengers and listening to the radio. No one beeped their horn or got out of their car. It was as if nothing out of the ordinary was occurring. Surrounded by people, they were utterly alone.

It was at that moment that Jonathan broke out of his stupor. The gap was almost wide enough for the giant to reach through. Despite the strain on his face, he was still grinning in triumph.

"It's me he wants! If I go, he'll follow me!"

As the man peeled off the door like he was opening a tin can, Jonathan unbuckled himself and slipped through the gap into the backseat. He opened the back door on the driver's side and with that he was out. The giant threw the door down onto the pavement, only to see Jonathan sprinting away on the other side of the car.

"Jonathan!" Mrs. Elwood screamed out of her window. "Run!"

He didn't need telling twice. Jonathan raced down the central lanes of traffic, protected by the massed ranks of stationary cars. He turned his head to check that Mrs. Elwood was safe, and was relieved to see that the giant had forgotten about the car and was walking unhurriedly after Jonathan instead. Slipping between two cars, he cut left and headed down a side street that led to the Thames waterfront. His attention firmly fixed on Humble, Jonathan didn't notice the black van parked on the side of the road. He didn't see the side door open and a small, bald man come bounding out. Nor did he see the woman dressed in a long black cloak with fluorescent yellow hair. He didn't notice any of this until it was too late.

Jonathan ran, crashing straight into Marianne's arms. At once that familiar intoxicating scent washed over him.

"Hello again, Jonathan. It's nice to see you again. We missed you last time."

He wriggled in her arms, trying to hold his breath. Beside him Skeet giggled and poked him sharply in the ribs.

"No way, heh, no way out this time, puppy."

The giant was catching up with them. If he got his hands on Jonathan, then he was doomed. Still writhing and kicking, Jonathan's hands scrabbled around for anything that might help him. His left hand closed around a chunk of Marianne's hair. He yanked as hard as he could, and she screamed in pain. Skeet threw his head back and screeched in sympathy. Jonathan seized the opportunity to kick him sharply in the shins and break away from the two of them. He spun off, down toward the Thames Path.

"Humble!" Marianne shouted, clutching her head. "Get him!"

Jonathan pounded along the Thames Path. The weather was bearing down, and the biting wind and rain had driven people off the streets and indoors. The river was at low tide, but under the bridges waves lashed at the struts. Globular lamps lined his route, giving the path a ghostly white hue. Behind him, Jonathan heard a sound and looked back over his shoulder. What he saw chilled him to the bone. The giant Humble had broken out of his slow shuffle into a full-pelt sprint. His long, spindly legs stepped into a spidery scuttle that ate up the ground and propelled him forward at an unnatural speed. Jonathan gasped and redoubled his efforts. As he ran, the metal girders of Blackfriars Bridge loomed into view.

He skidded to a halt at the base of the bridge, where the explorer Raphael Stevenson and Molly had come over a century before him. A metal staircase led up from the path and onto Blackfriars Bridge, which stretched out across the dark expanse of the Thames. The path continued underneath the bridge, and through an extended section of scaffolding. To his left, a ladder curled over the top of the riverfront wall and led directly to the bed of the Thames. Jonathan hurriedly glanced across. The tide was low enough for the muddy, stony bottom of the river to be visible at the edges of the waterway.

Jonathan hesitated, the wind whistling across his face. Up the stairs lay London, the city he knew, crammed with bright lights and crowds of people. If the book was right, down the ladder was a crossing point, and the unknown dangers of Darkside. The giant would be on him in seconds; he had to decide. . . .

With one last look at the London skyline, Jonathan hoisted himself up onto the top of the wall and began to climb down the ladder. The rungs were cold and slippery from the rain, and in his haste he lost his footing. His feet shot out into the air, and his arms yanked in their sockets as he gripped the rung. He had to cling on with all his might to stop himself from falling down to the riverbed. From somewhere back on the path he heard a distant shout from Marianne: "Don't let him get away!"

He clambered down to the bottom of the ladder and stepped down on the riverbed. The ground underneath his feet was muddy and treacherous, and at every footstep mud grasped at his legs, as if hoping to suck him down under the surface. Lifting his knees up as high as he could, Jonathan staggered away from the ladder and along the side of the wall. It was like trying to run through glue.

He looked up and saw Humble moving swiftly down the ladder after him. There was no telling what the giant might do if he caught him down here. Everything was black, the horizon dominated by the vast silhouettes of the bridge columns. There was no escape, no hiding place. Jonathan tried to move more quickly, but the mud was pulling him back, and he could feel his legs beginning to tire. Humble dropped lightly onto the riverbed and began to take purposeful strides in his direction. The mud was slowing him down too, but not by much.

The sound of traffic rumbling on the bridge overhead filled Jonathan's ears. Glancing around for an escape route, he saw that the low tide had revealed a small inlet pipe feeding into the Thames. A battered grille had fallen away from the entrance, and a stream of brown water trickled forlornly out of it. A couple of stones had collapsed, blocking off part of the opening, but there was just enough room for him to squeeze through. It was hard to believe that a secret world lay beyond this grimy maw.

Humble was only a couple of squelching footsteps behind him. Jonathan forced one last effort from his legs and waded over to the pipe. He tossed his backpack into the blackness and heard the splash as it landed. Getting a handhold on the inside of the pipe, he lifted himself up and through the entrance. The mud released his feet with a defiant sucking sound. Jonathan's body was now pressing down on his arms, and he had to wriggle like an eel to make any progress. The pipe sloped sharply upward, and it took the last reserves of strength in his body to scrape along it. The atmosphere was suffocating: There was hardly enough room to breathe, let alone to move. To make matters worse, scummy water soaked his face and seeped into his mouth.

A scrabbling noise came from near his feet. Twisting around, Jonathan could make out Humble's long arm slipping down the pipe after him like a python. There wasn't enough space for the giant to crawl after him, but he could still drag him out of the pipe. Jonathan cried out and forced himself deeper into the pipe, cutting his knee on a sharp edge in its concrete wall. His backpack was blocking the way, and he had to frantically shove it forward with his head.

The hand was almost upon him. Jonathan felt a fingertip brush his sneaker, and then suddenly the backpack popped out of the other end of the pipe, and with one final thrust he followed it. Jonathan hit the ground with a thump and lay still, his breath coming in hoarse gasps. He had made it.

Jonathan had come out in an underground circular chamber. Large gray pipes jutted out from the walls and spat streams of water into a dank pool at the heart of the room. A wide runoff channel then carried the water out of the chamber and away into the blackness. The roaring of the cascades hurt Jonathan's ears, and there was a stale smell in the air that stuck to his damp clothing. A ladder hung down from a small grille in the ceiling. Through the grille's thin bars a London street-light threw down a glowing orange lifeline. It provided the only light in the room.

Moving his limbs stiffly, Jonathan checked his possessions. Amazingly, despite his desperate scrabble through the pipe, his backpack hadn't been too badly damaged, although his clothes were soaked through. And he could still feel the knife in his pocket. But his cell phone wouldn't turn on and, even worse, the ink had run on the piece of paper with Carnegie's address on it. There was just an illegible smear. Jonathan slapped a hand to his wet forehead. How was he supposed to find this guy now?

He walked around the pool and climbed the ladder up to the grille. He was hoping that he could lift it up and get back onto the surface, but it was locked. There was no way back. Jonathan was about to slide down again when he heard a familiar, well-spoken female voice on the street above.

"So where's the boy, Humble?"

There was a brief silence.

"He made it through the pipe?" Marianne said incredulously.

Another silence.

"Why didn't you stop him?"

More silence.

"You want Skeet to chase after the puppy?"

"Is he still alive?"

"Can still smell him. Puppy not dead. Puppy *very* close."

"Is that so?" Marianne raised her voice. "Can you hear us, Jonathan? I bet you can."

Underneath the grille, Jonathan held his breath.

"You're a brave little one, aren't you? It's not over, though. If you're going to Darkside, we'll go too. You'll be a very long way from home, little one, and we know every street corner and back alley. There'll be no escape. . . ."

Jonathan was relieved to hear the whir of sirens approaching. Marianne turned back to her companions.

"I think that little show has attracted attention. Let's

get out of here. Oh, and Humble? You'd better start thinking of ways to break the news to Grimshaw."

At least he had given them the slip. All he had to do now was work out how to get out of here. Jonathan wiped a sleeve across his dripping nose and peered into the gloom. In the corner of the room a set of crumbling stone steps led down into a wide, arched passage propped up at regular intervals by rounded pillars. Amid the stillness the only sounds were the dripping of water, the squeak and rustle of rats, and — somewhere in the distance — the low, throaty rumble of an Underground train.

There didn't seem to be any choice. Jonathan hurried down the passage, choking on the foul stench of decay that rolled in waves toward him: the smell of sewers, toilet waste, and rotting rodent corpses. The floor was uneven and covered in a thin film of dank water, and the splashing sounds of his footsteps echoed off the curved walls. Jonathan clenched his fist in triumph when he spotted an iron spiral staircase at the end of the passage, flanked by a pair of gas lamps. Desperate for a taste of fresh air, he scampered up the steps. And with that, he came out on Darkside.

# 8

"So then, Ricky Thomas . . ."

Officer Ian Shaw burst into the briefing room slightly out of breath, spilling coffee from his Styrofoam cup on himself in the process. A crowd of people — a mixture of uniformed officers and plainclothes detectives — were seated on chairs and perched on desks in an informal semicircle. The scene looked more like a sixth-grade classroom than the heart of a massive police operation. At the front of the room, the captain stood next to a whiteboard covered in various photographs. He was clearly in the middle of a speech, and stopped pointedly as Shaw entered the room. Shaw cursed himself under his breath. If only he hadn't made that blasted coffee! The captain didn't tend to forget things like that.

"Sorry, Cap'n," he mumbled.

The captain glared at him.

Feeling everyone staring at him, Shaw shuffled red-faced through the ranks of officers to the back of the room. Even the aroma of stale cigarette smoke and sweat couldn't mask the sense of anticipation in the air. Every policeman in the room knew that this could be the case that made his or her career. One lucky break, one discovery, one arrest: That would be all it would take. There was more than enough media attention surrounding the case to guarantee promotions for those who did well. Even on a dreary Tuesday morning, there was a gaggle of reporters and photographers gathered around the entrance of the police station. Officer Shaw watched them from the window, chatting away on their cell phones under brightly colored umbrellas, and wondered what he would look like on television.

"Now that everyone's bothered to turn up . . ." said the captain. Shaw winced. "As I was saying, we're in a bit of a bind here, ladies and gentlemen. We need a quick result, or believe me, we're *all* going to get it in the neck." He took a pen from his top pocket and tapped the first photograph. "This unfortunate young man is thirteen-year-old Ricky Thomas. He travels down to London on a school trip. In the middle of Trafalgar Square he wanders off. No one has seen him since. Broad daylight in one of the most popular tourist destinations in the country, and no one sees a thing."

Officer Shaw took a sip from his coffee. It was scalding hot. With a great effort he managed not to yelp out loud, but his coughs and splutters still made the captain shake his head in disbelief. He moved on to the next photo on the whiteboard. "This is the only clue we've got, for all the good it's done us."

Shaw leaned in closer, struggling to see the photo.

"It was taken by a young Japanese woman at the scene. Now, she was in Trafalgar Square at the same time that Ricky disappeared, but she doesn't remember seeing him. However, if you look in the bottom corner of the photo, he's there."

It was definitely Ricky. He was scurrying toward the steps that led out of the square. His face was pale and there was a hunted look in his eyes. There were people all around him, but no one was taking any notice of him.

"The boy's clearly terrified. It looks like someone's after him. Could be bullies from his school. Could be something much worse than that. The thing I want you to think about is this — why doesn't he ask for help?"

The captain paused, and then referred to a sheet of paper.

"And last night we came across a bad traffic accident on Upper Thames Street that had ripped the passenger seat door right off a car. The driver says it was done by a man who was chasing after the son of a friend of hers: a fourteen-year-old named Jonathan Starling. So far we haven't been able to track down the kid, but he's got a history of truancy as long as your arm, so be careful not to make any assumptions. We're checking it out to see if there are any links, but our witness is flaky to say the very least."

Seemingly upset by the unfairness of it all, the captain sighed. These really were unusual incidents. With most child abductions there was usually a host of witnesses clamoring to give statements, especially in public places. Parents and teachers tended to keep an eye on anything looking suspicious involving children. Not this time, though.

"So, to conclude: We're in quite a mess. We've got two suspected abductions, neither of which we can be absolutely sure are actual kidnappings. They're also linked by the fact that a) both boys are roughly the same age, and b) there are no leads at all. We have to change b) in the next couple of days. The press are screaming for us to get a result, and saying that heads should roll if we don't. They have a nasty habit of getting their way, so keep your eyes and ears open for anything that might get our investigation going. It could be the smallest thing. The first thing I'm going to do is split you all into teams and send you back to the crime scenes. There's got to be something there, people!"

At that moment a young female officer stuck her head around the door. "Sorry, sir. Someone wants to speak to you. Says it's important."

The captain threw his hands up in exasperation and left the room. Noting the dark coffee stain on his tie, Officer Shaw slipped out after him and headed to the bathroom to splash some water on it. He had finished dabbing at the stain, and had just ducked into a cubicle, when he heard two men entering the bathroom. They were arguing, and with a jolt Officer Shaw recognized the captain's voice.

"You're darn right we're going to talk about it here!" he roared. "This is a terrible disgrace!"

"If you insist," a voice replied delicately. "There's not a great deal to talk about, though. The chief's asked me to take over operational responsibilities for the case. You'll stand down. That's it."

"And has the chief been kind enough to explain his reasons for this change?"

"With all due respect, I wouldn't have thought he'd need to. Two disappearances in two days, and you don't have a single clue to go on."

"That's because there *are* no clues to go on," retorted the captain. "I can't make things exist that aren't there. But with a bit of good old-fashioned police work, we'll turn something up. I know it!"

"Personally, I've never been much of a fan of old-fashioned things." There was a note of amusement in the other man's voice. "It is the twenty-first century, you know."

"That's why you're perfect to lead the Special Investigations Unit. No appreciation for proper police work. Spend all your time fooling around on the Internet and hobnobbing with the big shots. None of the cops in this station trust you, you know."

"I don't need them to trust me. I only need them to do what I say. I think my results speak for themselves. I'm not sure that the Biloxi brothers would have been caught with just 'old-fashioned police work.'"

"Everyone knows there was something fishy about that case," hissed the captain. "Don't think that we don't know what happened there."

"What exactly are you saying?" The amusement had abruptly disappeared from the man's voice. "That sounds remarkably like an accusation. A man in your position should be more careful about what he says, don't you think?"

The captain said nothing.

"Now, do you think we could go and tell your men about the situation? Or would you like me to personally deliver your letter of resignation to the chief?"

"This isn't over."

"You're quite right. It's just beginning."

The two men left the bathroom. Officer Shaw got up and hurriedly buckled up his pants. He shouldn't have heard any of that. Whatever was going on, it was pretty serious. The captain had never sounded that rattled before. He rushed out of the cubicle and back toward the briefing room, only to find himself late for the second time that morning. This time, the captain couldn't even be bothered to glare at him. Standing beside him was a sharply dressed blond man wearing a pair of sunglasses.

"All right, listen up! The chief's demanded some operational changes. He's brought in the Special Investigations Unit to work alongside us." He nodded at the blond man. "Carter Roberts, the head of the SIU, will now be heading up the case."

There was a murmur in the room. The SIU was an elite crime-fighting unit that had gained a fearsome reputation in the past couple of years. Big-name criminals, big-name busts. The capture of the Biloxi brothers, three siblings who had been terrorizing South London for decades, had been a real feather in their cap. If it was difficult to like them personally, their results demanded respect.

Carter Roberts stepped in front of the captain and addressed the room. "Thank you, Captain. I realize that this is a bit sudden, but I'm sure that we'll work things out quickly enough." He gave a dazzling smile. "Oh, just one more thing, sir. I'm going to need one of your men to personally assist me while I work on the case."

The room automatically stiffened to attention.

"Is there anyone in particular that you had in mind?"

Carter Roberts smiled and said, "I haven't worked with anyone here before, but I have been given one recommendation." He flicked through a spiral-bound notepad. "Ah, yes. I'll take Officer Shaw, if you don't mind."

The captain gaped at him. "Well, of course . . . I mean, anything that you need if . . . you know . . . if you're sure that you want him."

"Absolutely."

Officer Shaw gulped. Wherever the SIU went, danger followed hot on their heels. He was going to be close to the action, all right.

# 9

It wasn't what he had expected. It wasn't like anything he had ever imagined. Jonathan stood motionless, barely even breathing, and tried to take everything in. His senses were working overtime, struggling to make sense of the scene before him.

He had come out onto a narrow cobbled street that bubbled with a cauldron of voices: garbled shouts, throaty cries, squawks of protest, and snarled threats. A procession of horse-drawn carriages filed past in front of him, and Jonathan's ears reverberated to the rumble of the wheels and the loud clopping of hooves on the cobblestones. On either side of the street, a row of tall, soot-covered buildings leaned menacingly toward one another like boxers. Above their high arched roofs, towering chimney stacks punctuated the skyline, bellowing dense clouds of smoke that turned the air into a permanent night. A milky full moon shone weakly though the acrid haze.

Jonathan began to cough violently — whether from the smoke stinging his lungs or the foul stench that pervaded the sidewalks he wasn't sure. No one around him seemed affected by the atmosphere. Despite the late hour, the sidewalks were thronged with a mass of people ebbing and flowing in every direction. They were all dressed in old-fashioned clothing: the men in suits, long cloaks, and high stovepipe hats, and the women in ankle-length dresses and shawls. Jonathan couldn't help but gape at them. It was as if he had traveled back in time.

But as the passersby hurried under the faint illumination of the streetlamps, he realized that it wasn't just their clothing that was strange. Every now and then he caught a fleeting glimpse of something that unnerved him: a gentleman with red lipstick smeared over his mouth grinned at his companion, revealing a set of sharp, protruding front teeth; a woman with the vacant eyes of a sleepwalker wandered past, nails clawing at her exposed skin; from somewhere in the folds of a dress or the confines of a suit, a blade glinted evilly. Despite the pandemonium, the pushing and the jostling of the crowd, there were some whose path was always clear; space opened up magically around them. Jonathan realized that he was in serious danger.

It was tempting to go back into the passageway and hide, but he knew that somehow he had to find Carnegie. There was only one thing to do. He took several calming deep breaths and stepped out onto the street. Immediately the crowd swept him away. He fought to keep his feet, but at every step an elbow or a foot knocked him, and it was impossible to keep his balance. Storefronts streamed by so quickly that he didn't have time to see what they were selling. Street-sellers tried in vain to shout above the din, clinging on to the streetlamps to protect themselves from the swell of the crowd.

Jonathan's head spun as he tried to keep track of where he was. Two mongrel dogs began fighting in front of him, knocking him over as they rolled around in the dirt. He quickly tried to get up, but the crowd buffeted him, keeping him on the ground. Jonathan was starting to panic when a hand reached down and pulled him upright. A man dragged him into a quiet alleyway, away from the dangerous undertow of the crowd. He was dressed in an immaculately pressed three-piece suit, and his hair looked like it had been slicked down with gel.

"You all right there, boy? Bit of a close one, that."

"Yeah, thanks," Jonathan panted gratefully. "I couldn't get up."

"You look a bit lost, son. Can I help with anything?"

"I'm looking for a man named Carnegie. Do you know where he lives?"

The man's eyes narrowed, and Jonathan was suddenly aware that he was being held rather more firmly than necessary. "Carnegie? That name rings a bell. Hmm . . ."

As the man pondered the question, Jonathan felt a slight movement in his jacket. He looked down. To his horror, he saw that a withered third hand had appeared from inside the man's waistcoat, and was deftly rummaging through Jonathan's pockets! Jonathan cried out with shock and tried to back away, but the man had him in a strong grip, pinning his arms to his sides. As the third hand dug around for valuables the thief's eyes glanced nervously left and right.

"You're a bit of a prize, aren't you?" he muttered.

As he loomed closer Jonathan could smell the air of decay that hung off him. He shuddered, and again tried to wriggle free.

"There you are!" a girl's voice piped up.

Both Jonathan and the pickpocket whirled around and examined the source of the voice. She was small, maybe fourteen or fifteen, with fiery auburn hair draped artfully over one shoulder, and swathed in a heavy black cloak. Ignoring the thief's startled gaze, she pushed her way past him and poked Jonathan in the chest.

"Where have you been? I've been looking all over the Grand for you!"

"I . . . er . . ." stammered Jonathan.

"Stop stuttering!" the girl yelled. She turned to the pickpocket, who was looking uncomfortable with all the commotion, and gave him a sweet smile. "Thank you . . . Yann, isn't it? I remember seeing you up at the house. You were visiting my master. You do remember who *he* is, don't you?"

The man nodded sullenly.

"Then you wouldn't dream of hurting me. Or my brother. Because you know what would happen then, don't you?"

She actually batted her eyelids. The pickpocket sullenly relented, releasing Jonathan from his grip. The third hand withdrew back into his waistcoat. With a malevolent glare, he sloped away.

"Wow . . . thank you," said Jonathan. "That was incredible!"

When she turned around again, any trace of affection had disappeared from her voice. She spoke in a cold, urgent undertone. "Look, I don't know who you are, or what you think you're doing, but you're a dead man if you keep acting like that."

"Keep acting like what?"

"Like you don't know your way around. Like you're a fool."

"But I don't know my way around!" he replied helplessly. "What am I supposed to do?"

The girl was already striding away down the street. Jonathan raced after her.

"Hey . . . wait for me!"

She tutted with impatience. "Don't you have a home to go to or something?"

Jonathan grabbed her arm, forcing her to stop. "You know what? No, I don't. I've nearly been kidnapped, nearly drowned, and now I'm lost in this weird place where everyone wants to kill me. I could really do with a bit of help, you know?"

He was shouting now, past the point of caring whether anyone else was watching. The girl pursed her lips, and looked down at her feet. "And what do you think I can do to help you?" she asked finally.

"I'm looking for this guy called Carnegie. I've lost his address. Do you know him?"

"*Everyone* knows Carnegie."

"Do you know where I can find him?"

The girl squinted up at the moon. "This time of night, he'll probably be in his lodgings. Walk down the Grand for five minutes. Turn left on Fitzwilliam Street. Carnegie's place is on the second floor. If I were you, I wouldn't bother him right now, though."

"Thanks, but there's nowhere else I can go. I'm just going to have to risk it." He stopped, suddenly feeling awkward. "Look, my name's Jonathan and . . ."

But she was already walking away, calling out airily over her shoulder, "Good luck, Jonathan. Try not to get killed."

He thought about chasing after her again, but

the little redhead had already melted away into the crowd.

The walk down the Grand was the longest five minutes of Jonathan's life. It seemed to him that danger haunted his every step. Red-rimmed eyes shot hostile glances at him. Ugly, scarred faces broke into vicious smiles. Jonathan drew the hood of his jacket tightly around his face and kept his eyes fixed on the dirty sidewalk. At one point he slipped from the pavement into the gutter, and only just avoided being mown down by a horse-drawn carriage. The driver was whipping his steed furiously, and it whinnied and foamed at the mouth as it flew by.

By the time he came to a road branching off the Grand, Jonathan had been thoroughly shaken up. Above his head a battered street sign showed the letters FITZ. The rest was obscured beneath a coating of rust. A dirty poster had been stuck to the signpost, depicting two boys being ravaged by a pack of dogs, underneath the heading INCREDIBLE NEW ATTRACTION: LAST ANIMAL STANDING! From the other side of the street, there was a guttural roar and a scream. Jonathan took the hint and hurriedly turned left.

If the Grand was a feverish dream, then Fitzwilliam Street was a brooding nightmare. It was a narrow, winding road barely wide enough for a carriage to travel down. Shabby houses reared up on either side. The shopfronts bore the battle scars of war: Their signs had been ripped down, the windows smashed, and their doors kicked in. In one shop Jonathan could see the remnants of a small fire smoldering away in the back. None of the streetlamps here seemed to work, and he had to rely upon the moon for what little light there was.

Farther down the road he caught sight of a group of boys maintaining a sullen guard outside a shop marked DOONESBURY'S FUNERAL PARLOR. Although they were dressed in the old-fashioned clothing he had seen on the Grand, Jonathan guessed that they must have been about his age. They were taking turns throwing lit matches into the gutter, and there was an aggressive swagger about them that spelled trouble. As Jonathan scanned the scene, he caught sight of a sign hanging above the funeral parlor that said simply ELIAS

CARNEGIE. Great. If he wanted to get up there, he was going to have to get past the gang.

As he approached, a scuffle broke out as one of the boys decided to flick a match at one of the others. Jonathan tried to take advantage of the fracas to slip past, but they spotted him immediately and circled him like hyenas. The smallest boy — whose cocky manner suggested that he was the leader — reached up and poked him in the chest.

"Who are you?"

"I'm Jonathan."

"You're on our turf. People who come on our turf get hurt. Are you looking for a fight?"

Jonathan pointed to the sign above the funeral parlor. "I'm just going to see Carnegie," he said.

There was an audible intake of breath. The boys glanced at one another doubtfully.

"You don't know him," one of them sneered.

"Actually, he's a friend of mine."

"You're lying! He hasn't got any friends!"

"I'm going upstairs to see him. Do you want to come up with me and find out?"

Jonathan left the challenge hanging in the air. No

one said anything; then the leader of the gang slouched away down the road. "Come on. This is boring."

The rest of the boys followed him, elbowing their way past Jonathan. It seemed that knowing Carnegie's name wasn't such a bad thing around here. Now all he had to do was meet the man himself.

Jonathan slipped in through the front entrance and crept up a tired staircase. At the end of a landing there was a heavy red door that was covered in deep scratches. On the wall near it a brass plaque had been engraved with the words ELIAS CARNEGIE. PRIVATE DETECTIVE. Jonathan rang the bell but couldn't get any response, nor could he raise anyone by knocking. Eventually he tried the handle. It turned, and he entered the room.

Carnegie's lodgings were spare to say the least. No lights were lit, but Jonathan could make out two chairs and a low sofa positioned on a threadbare rug, and a rickety bookcase clinging to the wall. The fire had burned out in the hearth, and the room was deathly cold. Behind a long wooden desk there was a man slumped in a chair. He was facing away from Jonathan, staring out at the moon. Even in the gloom it was clear he was a broad, bulky man. When he eventually spoke, however, his voice was hollow and strained.

"What are you doing here?"

"I'm sorry . . . I did knock."

At the sound of Jonathan's voice, Carnegie turned around. His bulky silhouette seemed to fill the room. "I didn't say 'come in.' Basic manners, boy."

"Do you want me to wait outside?"

"I want you to go away."

Jonathan couldn't believe it. This was the person his dad had sent him to, the person he was relying upon to save his life. And now he was telling him to go away!

"But I need your help!"

"Not tonight, boy. Things are only going to get worse if you hang around."

"I've got nowhere to go!"

Carnegie leaped out of his chair and leaned over the desk. In the moonlight Jonathan could see that his eyes were filmy and bloodshot. "Do you not understand?" he hissed. He pointed at the window. "Have you not seen the moon? Do you want me to hurt you? Leave now!"

"I need your help!" Jonathan tried again, desperately. "My dad sent me here. . . . He says he knows you!"

Carnegie had fallen back into his chair and was cradling his head in his hands, moaning. He seemed sick. Then his shoulders began to shake, and Jonathan wondered whether he was crying. He edged toward him, his arms outstretched.

"Mr. Carnegie? Are you OK?"

He placed a hand on one of his broad shoulders. A low chuckle escaped from Carnegie. "Feeling better, boy," he muttered thickly. "Much better."

Carnegie's head suddenly snapped up toward Jonathan, who recoiled in horror. His face had undergone a terrible transformation. A gray matting of fur covered his skin, and his teeth had grown long and sharp. Where before his eyes had been those of a weak human's, now they were the blank, hungry eyes of an animal.

Jonathan backed away to the office door. Carnegie rose and moved powerfully after him. "I did tell you to leave."

"I'm going . . . I'm going!" Jonathan shouted.

He grinned, revealing the full horror of his incisors. "Too late now. . . ."

# 10

Carnegie hurled himself at Jonathan, his mouth wide open and his teeth gleaming. Jonathan barely had time to twist his body out of the way before a huge hand — now more of a paw than a hand — sliced through the space where he had been standing. The beast snarled and bore down on Jonathan, moving with a feral, muscular grace. He seemed to grow in stature as he moved, his shoulders broadening and his muscles rippling beneath his shirt.

Jonathan had to do something, or he was a dead man. His fingers hurriedly sought out the knife in his pocket. As the beast neared he lashed out, felt the blade brush against thick hair, and darted around the other side of the desk. Carnegie howled and wiped a fleck of blood away from his face with a hairy hand. A deep chuckle escaped from his throat.

"You're going to need more than that sewing needle to hurt me," he barked.

"Why are you attacking me? I came here for your help!"

"Right place, wrong time, boy."

Jonathan scanned the room for a bigger weapon. There was a poker propped up next to the hearth, but there was no way he could get past the beast to get his hand on it. He was trapped. Why on earth had his dad sent him here?

He didn't have time to think about anything else. With a rush Carnegie came after him again, leaping over the desk. Jonathan ducked underneath and began to scramble away, but Carnegie landed easily on all fours and was on his prey in a flash. Jonathan had one agonizing glimpse of the door before the beast stretched out a paw and swatted him in the stomach. Jonathan crashed to the floor, the wind buffeted out of him. There was a tearing pain in his side, and when he touched the wounded area, his palm came away hot and sticky with blood.

Carnegie howled — this time with pleasure. He skirted around the desk and began to advance slowly, enjoying the desperation of his prey. Jonathan pushed himself weakly across the floor on his back, his feet slipping on the tattered rug, his whole body trembling with fear.

"No need to rush," the beast said, his gray fur glinting in the moonlight. "It's still early."

"Don't hurt me! I'm Alain Starling's son!"

Carnegie shrugged. "And?"

A sob escaped from Jonathan. The pain in his side was getting worse, and he could see the trail of blood he had smeared across the floor. With a thud his head hit the wall behind him. There was nowhere left to go. His life was going to end here, in this small, dark room in the middle of his worst nightmare. The beast was standing directly over him, blocking out the moon, blocking out the light, blocking out everything. Carnegie roared, and closed in on Jonathan. . . .

Light. It was the light he noticed first. Not the brilliant white light of a heavenly afterlife, but a wan, yellowy sunlight trickling in through the window. Jonathan opened his eyes, blinking. The ceiling of the room was cracked and covered in patches of black mold. He craned his neck around to get a better sense of his surroundings, but the movement sent a bolt of pain down his side. Jonathan ran his fingers through the torn remnants of his sweater to see if his wound was still bleeding, but while he had been unconscious it had been dressed and bandaged.

"So you're awake."

Carnegie was sitting back in his chair, looking drawn and tired, but human. The hair had disappeared from his face, save for his unshaven chin, and his teeth had shrunk to normal size. He was wearing a long black morning coat over a grimy waistcoat covered in dark splotches of color. As he spoke he tapped a fountain pen on the desk and refused to look Jonathan in the eye.

"I guess so. What happened?"

"We both got lucky."

Jonathan moved into a sitting position, wincing in pain. "I don't feel very lucky."

"Believe me, you're the luckiest person in Darkside. And there's a lot of people here who know how to make themselves *very* lucky. Especially when I play cards with them."

"Eh?"

He snorted. "Forget it. How's the side?"

"It hurts like crazy."

"Yeah. It will for a bit. You'll live, though."

A glass of water had been set down by the sofa. Jonathan took a sip from it while Carnegie continued tapping the desk. If he didn't know any better, he would have said the detective was nervous. Carnegie shook his head with a rueful grin.

"So you're the Starling boy, then?"

Jonathan nodded. "I tried to tell you."

"Forgive me. I don't always think that clearly when I'm . . . well, you know, in the other form. And it's been a while since I saw your father."

"So . . . you're a . . ." Jonathan wasn't sure that he could bring himself to say it. "You're a . . . werewolf?"

Carnegie rubbed a hand over his face. "This is going to be a long day. I can sense it. Let's clear up one thing, boy. I prefer 'wereman.' Did you see me running around on all fours last night?"

"I guess not."

"I mean, I'm not an animal."

"But every time there's a full moon, you . . . change?"

"Or when something annoys me enough. And I should warn you, boy, all these questions are pushing me pretty close right now."

He muttered an oath under his breath. Jonathan took another sip of water and looked out of the window.

Fitzwilliam Street was busier now than it had been at night, but it wasn't any more pleasant. Water streamed across the pavement, carrying with it a film of scum and excrement. The Darksiders splashed their way through the muck, splattering it onto their clothing. Young boys in cloth caps and shorts darted across the road on mysterious errands, narrowly avoiding being trampled beneath thundering carriage wheels. Across the street, a man in a greasy white apron stood in the doorway of a butcher's shop, a cleaver resting menacingly in his folded arms. The sky was still overcast from the clouds of filth churning out from the industrial chimneys, and a pall of smoke from an unseen fire had drifted over from a nearby street.

"So why am I alive, then?"

"Hmm?"

"You forgot my dad's name. But you didn't kill me. Why not?"

Carnegie looked up for the first time. "You passed out, and this rolled out of your pocket." He held up a small object. It was the used bullet that Mrs. Elwood had given Jonathan! In the shock and the confusion he had forgotten all about it.

"*That* made you stop?"

"Might forget the odd name, boy, but I'll never forget that. This bullet would have ended my life many years ago had your dad not pulled it out of me."

"But I though werewo . . . weremen could only be hurt by *silver* bullets."

"You ever been shot, boy?"

"No."

"Still hurts pretty bad. Here." He tossed the bullet over. "You might want to keep hold of it. Just in case."

"So am I safe now?"

"From me. For now." Carnegie grinned. "There. Isn't that better?"

In the freezer room of the butcher's shop on Fitzwilliam Street, Jonathan watched in horror as Carnegie devoured a raw leg of lamb, his teeth greedily tearing strips of flesh off the bone. He didn't seem to notice the flecks of blood and skin falling onto his morning coat. Noting Jonathan's expression, Carnegie offered him the leg. "Are you sure you don't want some?"

"No, thanks."

"And you said you were hungry!"

"Yeah. I was. I don't think I am anymore."

Carnegie swallowed a large mouthful of meat. "I'm starving. I nearly ate last night, but, well, you know . . ."

Jonathan stamped his feet to try and shake off the cold. He had borrowed a shirt and pants from the wereman, rolling up the sleeves and cinching his belt tightly to try and fit into them, but it was still freezing. The meat cooler was a square room covered in white tiles. Huge racks of meat hung in rows from hooks, swaying from side to side. Carnegie hadn't changed his clothes — save for the addition of a stovepipe hat, rammed so far down his head it nearly touched his eyebrows — but he seemed unaffected by the temperature. His only thought was of the meat under his nose. Jonathan had feared that he was going to turn back into the vicious beast from the previous night, but if anything, the sight of a normal-looking man gobbling raw meat off the bone was even worse.

The cooler door opened, and the grim butcher stuck his head around the corner.

"How's the lamb?"

"Good as ever, Col. Boy doesn't seem to want anything, though."

The butcher shrugged. "Some people prefer their meat cooked, Carnegie. What can you do?"

"Eat them?"

The butcher let out a fat chuckle. "Are you out on a case? Do you want a bottle of your special recipe?"

Carnegie gave Jonathan a sly glance. "I think the boy might be trouble. Better get me a bottle, just in case."

The butcher elbowed his way between two huge sides of beef and lumbered over to the far corner of the room. He returned with a brown glass bottle encased in frost, and handed it to the wereman. Carnegie slipped it into the inside pocket of his coat. "Thanks, Col."

"Um, sorry, but . . . what is that?" asked Jonathan.

"That's Carnegie's Special Recipe. He never goes out on a case without it," Col explained.

"It's gotten me out of a few tight spots, I can tell you."

Jonathan frowned. "Why do you keep it in the freezer?"

"It's volatile stuff. Best kept frozen. One spark and it'll blow this place sky-high."

"What's *in* it?"

"Distilled human blood and rubbing alcohol," replied Col. Seeing the horrified look on the boy's face he laughed, and withdrew from the freezer.

Carnegie nudged Jonathan. "Just a little butcher's humor there, boy. Don't listen to him."

Jonathan smiled politely.

"So anyway . . . you came to me for help. From Lightside. You must be in pretty serious trouble."

"What's Lightside?"

Carnegie made a small sound of exasperation. "How did you find me? How did you survive the crossing here, when you seem to know absolutely nothing? Look, this part of town is Darkside. It stretches from Bleakmoor in the north to Devil's Wharf in the south. It's not much to look at, I'll grant you, but it's home. Lightside is . . . everywhere else. The other side of the coin. Where we don't go."

"I've never heard of it."

"Why does that not surprise me? Anyway, it's a Darksider term. You live in Lightside. So, to repeat my question: Why are you here?"

Jonathan's hands were turning blue from the cold. When he blew on them they ached. He started to speak, his teeth chattering.

"C-c-could we t-t-talk about this somewhere a bit w-warmer?"

Carnegie gave him a sympathetic look. "Of course, boy. Where are my manners?"

He hurled the ravaged leg of lamb into a corner and propelled his companion toward the exit. As they moved back through the warmth of the front of the butcher's shop, Jonathan plucked up the courage to whisper in his ear, "Um, Mr. Carnegie?"

"Just Carnegie'll do."

"You've still got blood on your chin."

"So?" Carnegie replied, and strode out into the busy daytime throng.

# 11

The Grand was as vibrant, filthy, and dangerous as it had been the night before. Carriages clattered down streets packed with Darksiders pushing and shoving past one another, quarreling with jabbing fingers and raised voices. For now the streetlamps were dull and lifeless, and the street was bathed in the murky yellow light of daytime. An electric crackle in the atmosphere suggested that a storm was brewing. Jonathan could feel the hairs rising on his arms. The tension had been transmitted to the inhabitants, and everywhere he looked he saw the potential for violence.

Carnegie strode on regardless, his gaze fixed directly in front of him. He was walking against the flow of the crowd, but space always appeared to open up in front of him. By contrast, Jonathan was knocked and buffeted as if he was standing in a gale. It was a constant struggle to keep up. Although everyone moved out of Carnegie's way, no one appeared pleased to see him. Jonathan noticed that people looked away from him, or down at their feet, as if they had spotted something fascinating on the pavement. Some failed to disguise their suspicion and outright hatred.

One drunken man, swigging unsteadily from a bottle of alcohol, barged into him as he passed. Carnegie didn't blink — but a large hand shot out and grabbed the man by the throat. He hoisted the drunk up and pinned him against a wall. The man's feet dangled uselessly in the air, searching desperately for the ground.

"You knocked into me," growled Carnegie.

The drunk stuttered an apology. Carnegie eyeballed him before relenting, and dropped the man in a choking heap onto the ground. Then he moved away, as if nothing had happened. Jonathan trotted after him.

"You see, boy, there're a few bad apples in Darkside. . . ."

"I can see that."

"But it's not so bad. All you have to do is set certain boundaries. Don't let anyone push you around. People respect that, after a while. Word gets around."

A massively obese woman appeared in front of Jonathan, rings of fat wobbling around her body like hula hoops. She leered menacingly and stretched out two fleshy arms, trying to envelop him in a bear hug, but he managed to evade her with a neat sidestep.

"Why is everyone so mean around here?" Jonathan panted, keeping one eye open for any more signs of trouble.

"Bad blood, boy. Bad blood. Our families used to live in your part of London too, you know. But many years ago, during the reign of that hag Victoria, the authorities decided to clean up the streets. Their gleaming city was too good for the likes of *us*. So they rounded up our grandparents —all the freaks, lowlifes, and criminals they could find — and herded them into this one area. We're their descendants. Everyone in Darkside has evil in their veins — some just have more than others."

"Is that why this place doesn't appear on any maps?"

Carnegie laughed scornfully. "Maps don't mean anything, boy. They're one side of the story, one person's view of events. You don't see Darkside on any maps? Of course you don't. The authorities don't want anyone knowing there's a whole world of danger on their nice, safe doorsteps. There would be total pandemonium."

He chuckled again, and Jonathan got the distinct impression that he would quite like that to happen.

"I don't get it, though," he confessed. "This is the middle of London. How can people not see all this?" He waved a hand around the Grand.

"Look, boy, if people try hard enough they can persuade themselves of pretty much anything. Most people don't want to acknowledge that Darkside exists, so they keep their heads down and carry on with their little lives. It's obvious we're here, but you need to look in the right places. You'll find that if you walk down a certain tunnel, or go down a certain staircase, or cut through a certain alleyway, *we're just around the corner.*" His eyes gleamed with mischievous intent.

In the middle of the Grand there was a large black statue on a plinth. It depicted a tall figure whose face was obscured by a thick coat and a low-brimmed hat. In one hand he carried a sharp, narrow blade.

Carnegie nodded at the statue. "That there's the founder of Darkside," he said. "The Ripper."

Something clicked in Jonathan's brain. "What, *Jack the Ripper*?"

"That's the man."

"I've read about him. He killed all these women in London, and they never caught him!"

"Not exactly caught, no. Instead, they had a word in his ear and sent him here to rule over Darkside. The authorities figured he was the only thing evil enough to stop this place from descending into complete anarchy. They were right too. Jack's grandson Thomas Ripper runs the place now. Don't see that much of him these days, but he's still the boss, all right."

Jonathan gaped. "Darkside's ruled by Jack the Ripper's family?"

"And you wonder why everyone's mean around here. Come on."

A crowd had gathered around the gutter by the side of the road and was roaring with excitement. Jonathan stood on his tiptoes, trying to see what was going on. Through a sea of waving arms he could make out two fighting cocks pecking and clawing at each other. Their feathers were soaked in blood. As the fight continued the shouts of the crowd spiraled louder and louder. Notes and coins changed hands with lightning speed as people bet on the outcome. Jonathan looked away. A woman in the crowd, clearly relishing the savage spectacle, had reminded him of something.

"Carnegie, have you heard of a woman called Marianne?"

"Marianne? Pale woman with fluorescent hair? She's a bounty hunter. She can hunt down anyone — for the right price, of course. How do you know about her, boy?"

"She's been trying to kidnap me. She's the reason I came to you."

The wereman raised a shaggy eyebrow. In the gutter, the crowd gave a final roar as one of the birds went down. "You should be honored. Marianne doesn't come cheap, and she tends to get her man. Someone really wanted to get their hands on you."

"Why would anyone here want to kidnap me? I'm not worth anything."

"That's the first sensible question you've asked. I'm not sure yet." Carnegie scratched his arm thoughtfully.

"One thing's clear, though. If Marianne has been hired to kidnap you, she won't stop until she does. We're going to have to be on our guard. First things first. You need to start trying to fit in a bit more. You're sticking out like a sore thumb at the moment. We don't tend to see many Lightsiders on these streets, and those we do aren't welcomed with open arms. Believe it or not, boy, you're something of a rarity."

"But if I can make the crossing over here . . . surely other people can too?"

"They can try. It's complicated."

"I can vouch for that," said Jonathan meaningfully.

"It's often tough physically, but it's more than that. To come to Darkside you've got to *think* differently. There's so much evil in the air that you've got to open your mind to it all, or it'll drive you insane. Most people can't cope with it. They break down, go crazy . . . it's not pretty."

Jonathan cast his mind back to Alain's ward and the deranged patients that wandered the halls there. "My dad's always getting sick."

Carnegie grimaced. "I'm not surprised. Alain used to spend a lot of time here."

"Hang on a sec. If coming over here caused his darkenings, why has he sent me here?" A wave of panic swept over Jonathan. "Does he want me to end up like that?"

"Well, that's hardly going to be a problem for you, is it? If you're part-Darksider, then crossing over isn't going to affect you at all."

Jonathan came to an abrupt halt. The shouts and oaths of the Grand faded into the background, and all the elbowing and jostling on the sidewalk left him unmoved. The only thing he could feel was the relentless pounding of his heart. "What did you say?"

Carnegie started to repeat himself, but saw the look on the boy's face and trailed off.

"You're saying I'm part-Darksider?" Jonathan asked in a quiet voice.

"Well, yes . . . but, your mother . . . you know . . . Has Alain not explained any of this to you?"

"You knew my mother?"

The wereman nodded sadly.

"Tell me everything you know about her!" Jonathan said urgently. "You have to tell me everything!"

Carnegie shook his head again, and was just about to reply when an open-top carriage drew up alongside the pair of them. A small, ratty-looking man hopped down from the driver's seat and gave Carnegie a broad grin. The detective sighed, and turned to Jonathan. "This is not going to be good news," he muttered.

The man sniffed, and drew his sleeve across his nose. "Vendetta wants to see you," he said.

Carnegie shrugged. "Tell him I'm busy, Luther."

The man opened the carriage door behind him and gestured inside. "He's waiting for you up at Vendetta Heights."

"All right. But I've got to take the kid with me," Carnegie responded.

It was Luther's turn to shrug. Jonathan grabbed the wereman and hissed in his ear, "Who's Vendetta?"

"You don't want to know."

"What happened to not letting anyone push you around?"

"You tend to make exceptions for Vendetta. Now shut up and get in, boy."

# 12

Ricky opened his eyes, and then immediately wished that he hadn't. There was a horribly bitter taste in his mouth, and it felt like someone was crashing a set of cymbals together inside his head. He reached up and gingerly touched a swelling on his forehead. Just the brushing of his fingertips made him wince. All in all, he felt in dreadful shape.

He was sitting on the floor of a metal cage, suspended from the ceiling of a cavernous hall by a chain attached to an iron hook. Even in the gloom, he had a sense of imposing vaulted walls rising up around him, as if he were in some sort of dark cathedral. His cage creaked with every draft of air. Ricky whimpered softly under his breath. Where on earth was he? The last thing he remembered was being chased through Trafalgar Square and hiding out in that church, and then he had met that woman. . . . It all seemed so unreal, like a bad dream. But now he was hanging in a cage, and it was only too real. A detached voice in Ricky's head was surprised that he had taken things so calmly. Perhaps he was in shock.

Either it was late at night, or the hall had no windows, because it was difficult to make out anything in the darkness. From the odd tortured groan of metal he got the impression that there were more cages gently shifting in the air alongside his, although how many, and how far the hall stretched on for, he couldn't be sure. Faint rustles and mutters floated up from the floor, suggesting that there were more people down there. Although a filthy blanket had been left lying on the floor of the cage, it was stiflingly hot. Ricky unzipped his coat and used it as a makeshift pillow. He may have only just woken up, but his head hurt so much and the situation seemed so hopeless that all he wanted to do was fall back to sleep.

He wasn't to be that lucky. At that moment a shaft of light appeared on a wall far down below, briefly revealing several stacks of large cages on the hall floor. Inside the cages, animals shied away from the light. Then two figures padded into the room. One was a thin man carrying a flaming torch above his head like an umbrella. The other, her hair glimmering in the torchlight, was his kidnapper. Instinctively, Ricky shrank away from the light source. He needn't have bothered. The man and the woman were focused firmly on each other. Despite the fact that they were speaking in hushed tones, it was clear that they were arguing.

"I don't need a bounty hunter to tell me how to count, Marianne. I asked for two half-Darksiders, and you've only given me one."

The man's voice was as parched as dried bones. Every syllable rasped against the back of his throat like sandpaper. Marianne poked him angrily in the chest. "And I don't need a pet shop owner to tell me about bounty hunting, Grimshaw. I've given you everything that was available."

"A pet shop owner?" His voice rose in indignation. "I am a collector, a scientist, an entertainer! I bring the strangest and most exotic creatures from Lightside and display them here. They fight; they kill; they die. People travel from far and wide to see me. The Beastilia Exotica is the jewel in Darkside's crown!"

With a flourish, Grimshaw whirled the torch around

the room. The light shimmered over more cages. It startled a mangy wildcat, which swung a futile paw through the bars of its cage. As Ricky looked on, he noticed narrow pairs of eyes glinting in the darkness on the other side of the hall, and realized that the space was crammed with captive animals. And him.

He shivered, and reached for his blanket.

"OK. Whatever. The fact is, you have a half-Darksider that you didn't have before."

"Marianne, I have been advertising this show for months. It is supposed to be the greatest spectacle ever staged at the Beastilia Exotica. The climax of the show is two half-Darkside boys fighting a pack of starved jackals. *Two* boys. That's what the posters say. Not one, two."

"So you've got one less. Who's going to care?"

"These things are very finely balanced. The jackals will polish off one boy in less than a minute. The audience will be unhappy." Grimshaw drew himself up. "I have a reputation to maintain."

"Well, it's not all bad news. We think the second boy's managed to cross over to Darkside."

"Shouldn't that make things a little easier for you? Surely even you can't fail to get him now."

"If he's not dead already, Skeet will track him down," came the icy reply. "He's hunting for the boy's scent as we speak."

"I don't know how you can trust that strange little creature."

"That 'strange little creature' is the only reason I can collect the little ones. Skeet can follow the scent of Lightside blood better than anyone else. That's why you hired me, or have you forgotten that?"

"And the giant mute?"

Marianne shrugged. "Size comes in handy sometimes. And I feel responsible for the way that Humble is. It seems only fair that I should look after him."

Grimshaw chuckled: a thin, tearing sound. "And you call *me* a pet shop owner."

"Enough, Grimshaw. I've had a busy few days, and I'm tired. This hasn't exactly been my favorite job, and I want my payment."

"Feeling sorry for the children? Maybe you *are* too well bred to be a bounty hunter after all."

Marianne let out a lazy sigh. "People have said that to me before, you know. Some of them even lived to regret it. Now, are you going to pay me the money you owe me, or do I tell Wren to go and cut the cage down?"

Ricky squeaked with panic, and both heads arced up toward his cage. He scrabbled away from the bars and hid under the blanket.

"Either you've got rats in your collection, or the little one is awake."

"I sold the last giant Sumatran rat years ago."

Through the gaps in the floorboards, Ricky could see Grimshaw looking up at him. The torchlight played across his face, revealing translucent, papery skin that barely covered his skull. His eyes were different colors: one green, one blue. He looked more disturbing than anyone Ricky had ever seen.

"Stay still up there!" he rasped. "You're a valuable commodity, and I don't want you getting injured."

Surprising himself, Ricky summoned the courage to answer back. "W-where am I? What do you want with me?"

"Try not to worry, little one," Marianne called back. "It will all be over very soon."

Ricky could feel waves of panic and anger

swelling within him. "What will be over soon? What am I doing here?"

Grimshaw grinned hideously. "You're backstage at the Beastilia Exotica. With all the other animals. Make the most of the glorious scenery — you haven't got much time left to enjoy it."

"But I'm not an animal! I don't want to be here — you can't keep me here! Let me out!" screamed Ricky. Fury at the injustice of it all rose up like vomit through his system and made his face burn red. He began rattling the bars, sending the cage swinging violently through the air. "LET ME OUT!"

Beneath him, a guttural chorus of barks, squeals, and howls broke out in sympathy, and the hall shuddered with the sound of the animals' protests. Marianne shifted uncomfortably from one foot to the other and looked away. "Come on, Grimshaw," she said. "Let's get out of here."

With that, the bounty hunter swept out of the hall. Grimshaw gave Ricky one last warning glance. Then, abruptly, he doused the torch in a bucket of water, plunging the room back into darkness.

# 13

The carriage moved smoothly off the Grand and the horses began clopping northward. Jonathan's mind was racing, and he was desperate to ask about his mother. Twice he opened his mouth, but both times Carnegie growled at him to keep quiet. It appeared questions were going to have to wait until later. Instead he stared out through the window at his surroundings. The streets became progressively quieter, though the air of poverty and decay never went away entirely. Packs of children in tattered clothes roamed the area, running alongside the carriage with their palms outstretched, pleading for money. Every so often Jonathan caught a glimpse of a house on fire, or a body lying prone in an alleyway. The carriage rattled on regardless.

Eventually the streets began to broaden and tall trees lined the road, the first Jonathan had seen in Darkside. The wind had picked up, and their brown and brittle leaves rustled uneasily in the breeze. The tightly packed rows of decrepit buildings had given way to luxurious mansions that hid behind high hedges and spiked railings. The road reeked of money.

Carnegie noticed Jonathan's inquiring gaze. "This is Savage Row. The richest people in Darkside live here. And Luther, of course."

He patted the driver on the back, a little too hard for it to be a friendly gesture. Luther flew forward and hauled on the reins, halting the carriage. He spun around angrily.

"You shouldn't push me, dog boy. You might not make it to Vendetta's, at this rate."

The burly wereman laughed in response. "Nonsense! We're nearly there. Come on. You're not going to keep him waiting, are you?"

Luther glared at him, and then reluctantly spurred on the horses again. The carriage swung swiftly around the winding bends of Savage Row, and Jonathan noticed how the street was getting steeper and narrower. The mansions had disappeared from sight, and the trees had closed in on all sides, forming a sinister guard of honor. It was getting colder now, and Jonathan pulled a blanket over his legs. Carnegie gave him a grim smile, but said nothing. He was looking tense.

The road abruptly leveled out and came out onto a wide, broad avenue. Here the trees were almost tall enough to block out any light from the murky sun. Nothing moved, and there was no sound except for the horses' urgent progress across the cobblestones. The avenue led to a set of imposing stone gates, which were being slowly strangled by green fingers of climbing ivy. Behind the gates, Vendetta Heights lay in wait for them.

It was a vast, brooding structure. The brickwork was old and coated with moss and shadow. Rows of elegant arched windows looked loftily down. Gargoyles perched in the eaves, their faces contorted into permanent stony leers. On the east wing of the mansion a spindly tower poked the sky. No lights could be seen anywhere, giving the building the air of an ancient mausoleum.

As the carriage approached, two shadowy figures emerged from the grounds of the house and opened the gates. Then they melted away into the undergrowth, as if fearful of being seen up close. The carriage rolled up the lengthy gravel driveway, skirting around an ornate fountain topped with a statue of a small child crying. Water spurted out from the child's eyes and trickled gently into the pool beneath its feet.

"Vendetta wants you to meet him in the greenhouse," said Luther, bringing the carriage to a halt. "It's around the back."

He cast another malevolent glare at Carnegie, who grinned. "Always a pleasure, Luther."

It had started raining gently. Judging by the color of the sky, it was late afternoon. Jonathan had lost track of what time it was. It didn't seem to make much difference in Darkside. You were only ever five minutes away from trouble, and that was the only thing that mattered. As Luther drove the carriage away, he and Carnegie followed a path that cut around the side of Vendetta Heights.

The grounds running off behind the mansion were as imposing a sight as the house itself. They must have covered a couple of square acres, before ending at a small forest that appeared to mark the end of the estate. Someone had lavished a great deal of attention on the lawn, cutting and trimming until it resembled an immaculate green carpet. A network of gravel paths ran across it, linking different parts of the estate. In the far corner of the lawn an intricate maze had been fashioned from dark green hedges. Despite the beauty of the view, there was a silent starkness about it that chilled Jonathan to the bone. There wasn't a sound, neither the chirp of a bird nor the rustle of an animal in the undergrowth. Carnegie seized the opportunity to lean over and speak in Jonathan's ear. "Vendetta's a banker, and the richest man in Darkside. He's also one of the most dangerous. I don't know why we're here, but it probably means we're in trouble. Keep your mouth shut, boy. And if I shout 'move,' don't stop running. Ever."

Jonathan nodded. There didn't seem to be anything he could say.

The greenhouse was a circular white building that stood alone on a terrace several levels lower than the mansion. As they wound their way down toward it, Jonathan could see a figure leaning casually in the shelter of the doorway. He was a tall, handsome man dressed in a three-piece suit with a dark red waistcoat. His skin was pale, and his hair so fair as to straddle the boundary between blonde and white. A pair of sharp half-moon spectacles pinched his nose. He straightened as they approached and spread out his arms in a welcoming gesture. His smile was as cold as death.

"Carnegie! Welcome to Vendetta Heights. You haven't been here before, have you?"

Carnegie doffed his hat. "No. I think I lost my party invitation."

"Still the same biting wit, I see. For once, though, you don't appear to be alone. Who's the boy?"

"Name is Tobias. His father hired me to find him. Only, when I do, he decides he can't afford to pay me. So I have to hold on to the boy until he changes his mind."

Vendetta ran an appraising eye up and down Jonathan, who shivered. "Cut off one of the boy's hands and send it to his father. That should speed up the process." He paused, and smiled again. "Sorry, Tobias, but business is business. Anyway, why don't the pair of you come inside? I fear the weather is going to break."

The greenhouse was hot and damp, and immediately Jonathan could feel beads of sweat forming on his forehead. Tropical plants and flowers crowded around on all sides, flashes of brilliant reds, blues, and yellows standing out among the heavy ferns. A small stream trickled in and out of the soil beds, before running off into the unknown. In the middle of the greenhouse there was a raised patio scattered with wicker chairs. Vendetta sat down in one and removed his spectacles.

"Bit warm in here, isn't it?" asked Carnegie pointedly.

"These flowers are probably as valuable as the Grand itself. It's worth my while to look after them. Sit."

It was more of an order than a request. Perspiring heavily, Jonathan did as he was told. A sweat patch was already forming on his back. Fitting awkwardly into a chair beside him, Carnegie was looking uncomfortable too. Only Vendetta remained unruffled by the heat. He doused a purple orchid with a water sprayer, before returning his attention to his guests.

"So you're probably wondering why I called you here."

"The thought had crossed my mind, yes," the were-man replied.

"Truth is, I need your help."

The shock must have been plain on Carnegie's face, because Vendetta burst into a peal of laughter. The shrill sound echoed off the greenhouse's roof panels. "Come on, it's not that amazing. Even the best of us need a hand from time to time."

"You could afford to hire anyone you want. Why me?"

"How should I put this? Word spreads about the . . . *effectiveness* of your approach. And I do so enjoy your company. I don't have any pets, you understand."

Vendetta clearly relished goading Carnegie. Though everything he said was delivered in a light, careless tone, the words were intended to cut and wound. Jonathan remembered the look in Vendetta's eyes when he had suggested cutting off one of Jonathan's hands. It had been devoid of any emotion, save for utter malice. Any involvement with this man would be a perilous affair. Carnegie was certainly unnerved by his proposition. He scratched his head vigorously. "What do you want me to do?" he asked, finally.

"I want you to find something for me."

"What? A gem? A weapon? An enemy?"

"A boy." Vendetta looked Jonathan straight in the eye. "A boy from Lightside named Jonathan Starling."

# 14

Jonathan froze in his seat. Despite the oppressive heat in the greenhouse, a sliver of ice ran down his spine. Vendetta kept his light blue eyes trained on Jonathan. In the silence, the trickling of the stream sounded like the roar of a waterfall. He forced himself to meet Vendetta's gaze as steadily as possible. If he looked guilty, he was done for. Thank God he had changed out of his normal clothes.

Though Carnegie must have been as stunned as Jonathan, he hid it well. His head was bowed, as if he were deep in thought. Eventually he looked up and cleared his throat.

"That doesn't sound like the sort of thing I usually do."

"It's not the sort of thing that I usually ask for. Terribly exciting, isn't it?"

"I'm not going over to Lightside."

"I'm not asking you to. The boy's here."

Carnegie snorted. "A Lightside boy? Here? I doubt that. Even if he did manage to cross over — for whatever reason — he'd be dead by now."

"Maybe. Maybe not. But I've got a feeling that he's still very much alive."

Again Vendetta's gaze flicked back to Jonathan, whose head was spinning with questions. How did the richest man in Darkside know his name? What did he want with him? Was it just a coincidence that he wanted to hire Carnegie, or did he know that his target was sitting directly in front of him? The sweat was now pouring down Jonathan's face. He hoped that Vendetta would chalk it up to the heat.

"OK, say the boy's still alive and I track him down. What do you want with him?"

"That's none of your concern. I'm only asking you to deliver him to me."

"I don't know . . ." the wereman said dubiously. "It all sounds a bit strange to me."

A look of exasperation flashed across Vendetta's face. "Look, Carnegie, it's not that difficult. Do you want the case or not?"

"I couldn't have a drink while I'm thinking about it, could I?"

Vendetta's jaw tightened. He eyeballed Carnegie for several seconds, before forcing his mouth to relax into a smile. "Of course. Let me just ring for the maid."

He rose smoothly from his chair and moved over to a table on the far edge of the patio, where an old-fashioned phone was obscured by a voluminous fern. He picked up the receiver without bothering to dial and spoke in a curt manner.

"Raquella, I'm in the greenhouse. Bring me a new bottle and another two glasses."

Carnegie raised an eyebrow as Vendetta hung up. "A phone in the greenhouse?"

"A necessary extravagance. I conduct a lot of business here. . . . Oh, I should have asked. Does the boy want anything? He looks a little flushed."

Carnegie's head spun around a little too quickly.

"No, no . . ." Jonathan cut in hastily. "I'm a bit hot, but I'm not thirsty at all."

The truth was, his mouth was parched and his throat was sore, but he didn't want to attract any more attention to himself. If he had to drink a glass of water, he wouldn't be able to stop his hand from shaking.

"Don't worry about him, Vendetta. He'll be fine. As soon as his father pays up, he can go home and drink all the water he wants to."

Vendetta laughed. "And you wonder why I want to hire you?"

"I guessed it was because of that business with McIlroy. . . ."

The two men began reminiscing over old Darkside feuds, and Jonathan felt himself slip out of the limelight. He found it strange to watch the two of them talking. Although the suave businessman and the shabby private detective were very different people, they were inextricably linked by the seedy world they lived in. They may not have liked each other but there was something between them, a grudging respect for each other's power.

Then Jonathan heard the door to the greenhouse gently open and close. He watched as a small girl appeared from between two large palm trees, balancing a drinks tray expertly in one hand. She was wearing a black dress and a white apron, which contrasted sharply with her flaming red hair. Even from a distance, Jonathan couldn't fail to recognize her. It was the girl who had saved him on the Grand. Which meant that she knew his name and, in all probability, he was done for.

"Ah, Raquella. Just leave the drinks over there, please."

She curtsied neatly and did as she was told. Jonathan held his breath. All he needed was for her to look up and say his name, and the game would be up. Luckily for him, she kept her eyes respectfully down and didn't look at either of the guests. Vendetta poured out a glass for Carnegie and handed it to him. The wereman took a long, messy swig, sending a spray of liquid down the front of his shirt. Vendetta shuddered, and took a delicate sip. The maid turned to leave, and was nearly out of sight before her master called her back. Jonathan's heart sank.

"Oh, Raquella. I think you know Carnegie."

She nodded, blushing, and smiled shyly at the

wereman. He gave her a cheery wave in return. "Hello there, little miss. How's your mother and father doing these days? I haven't seen them for a while."

"They're well, Mr. Carnegie. Thanks to you."

"Good. Tell them I said hello."

Vendetta smiled idly, and poured himself more drink from the bottle. "And have you met Mr. Carnegie's hostage, Tobias, Raquella?"

At last, her gaze fell upon Jonathan. Immediately there was a flicker of recognition on her face. Luckily for both of them, Vendetta's back was still turned. Jonathan nodded politely, and tried to look at ease. Carnegie must have sensed what was going on, because he glanced at Raquella and placed a finger over his lips.

Quickly recovering her composure, she gave a slight nod. "Hello, Tobias. You are lucky to have such an honorable kidnapper."

"I don't feel that lucky. He's already tried to eat me," Jonathan replied, truthfully.

Vendetta clapped with delight. "The boy has some spirit, after all! I thought he was just going to sit there and sweat! You may go now, Raquella. I think you have made enough of an impact."

The girl's cheeks reddened again, and with a curtsy she hurried out of the greenhouse. Carnegie took another long sip as Vendetta turned to face him. "So then, wereman. You've had enough of my drink. Are you going to take my case or not?"

"I'm not sure I can refuse. I'll take it."

"I always thought there was a brain rattling somewhere inside that head of yours. That's a wise choice. Come here. I've got something I want to show you."

Vendetta beckoned conspiratorially, and moved off the patio into the undergrowth. In this part of the greenhouse the plants had wrestled free from the confines of their soil beds, and long vines covered the concrete floor. Foliage closed in above their heads. Jonathan was suddenly very glad of Carnegie's presence in front of him.

They came out by an ornamental pool that had been dug into the floor, its surface flat and blank. Next to the pool there was an iron bench, perhaps placed there so that people could enjoy the peace and tranquillity of the setting amid the plants. The current occupant of the bench wouldn't have appreciated it, though. He was dead. The corpse was propped up on the bench, his limbs twisted into stiff contortions. His face had

161

turned bone white, and his mouth was wide open in an eternal scream. However he had died, he had suffered first.

Jonathan gasped. He had never seen a dead body before. The posture reminded him of his dad after a darkening, only this man was never going to wake up. Carnegie gripped his shoulder tightly in support, and moved ever so slightly in front of Jonathan. Vendetta walked calmly over to the bench and shook his head with mock remorse. He then began spraying a leafy plant behind the corpse's head.

"I wanted this man to work for me — made him a very generous offer, in fact — but he refused. Said that he was worried about the *responsibility*. Honestly. I tried to change his mind, but he wouldn't listen."

"So what did you do to him?" It was Jonathan who asked the question, his voice trembling.

Vendetta turned to him and smiled, revealing a set of long, sharp fangs. "What did I do? I sliced him open and drained every last drop of blood from his body. It wasn't much of a meal, Tobias. He was a rather scrawny character."

Jonathan stepped back in horror. His knees felt weak and there was a surge of nausea in his belly. Vendetta watched him struggle with undisguised amusement. "Now, Carnegie. That is most unfair. You're one of the few people who know about my condition. You might have warned the boy."

"Why are you showing us this? Is it a threat?"

"No. It's a guarantee." Menace flashed in Vendetta's eyes. "You cross me, you will pay for it. You, the boy, anyone I feel like blaming. Are we clear?"

Carnegie nodded.

"Good. Then bring me the Starling child. You can leave now."

With that he turned his back and resumed his spraying, humming a strange tune quietly to himself.

Although the sky was black and fat raindrops were falling across the grounds of Vendetta Heights, it felt good to be out of the greenhouse and in the open air. Jonathan's shirt was dripping with sweat, and the cool air on his back was a blessed relief. He stretched out his arms and spun around slowly as Carnegie closed the greenhouse door behind him. It was a total shock when the wereman grabbed him roughly by the collar and hauled him up into the air.

"What . . . have . . . you . . . done?" he hissed through clenched teeth.

"Oww! I don't know! Carnegie! Let me down!"

"WHAT HAVE YOU DONE?" Carnegie roared again. His eyes glittered with feral intent.

"I don't know! Shhh! He'll hear you!"

Carnegie blinked, and abruptly dropped Jonathan in a heap on the ground. The wereman spat out a curse and rubbed his head furiously, thinking hard. "OK. Not the boy's fault," he muttered to himself. "Don't blame the boy. Come on. We have to get out of here."

He hauled Jonathan up onto his feet, and propelled him back up the terrace and toward the front of the house. Jonathan's eyes were still watering from Carnegie's attack, and he stumbled with the fast pace. "Why did you do that? You're supposed to be my protector!"

The wereman stopped in his tracks. He sighed. "Look, boy, I'm sorry. I've got a few rough edges. In fact, I haven't really got any smooth ones. My job demands it. Things are going to get pretty hairy around here, and I need to know what's going on. Like, what Vendetta wants with you."

"I told you, I don't know!"

"Well, we need to find out, boy. Crossing that man is like signing your own death warrant. Come on. We need to get out of here. He might figure us out any second."

As they passed by the front of the house and started down the long driveway leading out of the grounds, Jonathan detected a movement coming from one of the rooms on the top floor of Vendetta Heights. There was a flash of red hair — Raquella was watching them leave. For a reason that he couldn't explain, Jonathan waved up at her. There was no reply, and the curtain was drawn swiftly across the window. In the background, there was a loud rumble of thunder.

# 15

"So what are your thoughts about the boys, then, sir?"

Officer Shaw and Carter Roberts were sitting in a high-class restaurant near Green Park tube station, one looking uneasy and on edge, the other a study in elegance. Roberts didn't bother to look up from the menu.

"What boys?"

"You know. Thomas and Starling."

"Oh, yes. Well, you know, it's still early. . . ."

"I just thought that you might have some initial suspicions."

"My suspicions are that it's going to take a long time for our meals to arrive. That's the only thing that's concerning me at this moment in time. I'm remarkably hungry."

The table fell silent again. If he was being honest with himself, Officer Shaw would have had to admit that working for the SIU had not been the thrilling experience he had anticipated. Ever since his selection, he had spent his nights dreaming about speeding around London in fast cars in hot pursuit of villains, or being involved in dramatic standoffs with the kidnappers on the top of high-rise buildings. The actual days had proved altogether less glamorous. Shaw chauffeured Roberts around the city in random, unexplained patterns, zigzagging from expensive clothes shops to hulking warehouses to deserted fairgrounds. They never seemed to spend more than a minute at a time in the open air, and Shaw was never allowed to follow his boss out of the car. Yesterday he had been forced to wait for several hours outside a run-down building in East London while Roberts had had his hair cut. It had been embarrassing to say the least, especially as Shaw had been unable to detect any difference in his hairstyle.

As far as actual police work went, there hadn't been any. The new searches at the kidnapping sites had turned up nothing. At Trafalgar Square one officer had found a strand of fluorescent orange hair, but Roberts had dismissed it on the spot.

"Of course!" he mocked. "The famous kidnapping clowns! Come on, everyone, you can do better than that."

He threw Shaw an exasperated glance. The officer forced a smirk back. The team had so few clues it seemed strange to ignore anything, but then he supposed that Roberts knew what he was doing. He just wished that he could see some evidence of it.

"So how are you faring down in the SIU, Shaw? Any problems?"

"No, sir. It's been fine. Only . . ."

"Only what?"

Shaw took a gulp from his water. "I just . . . I mean, I haven't really *done* anything yet. Apart from drive."

Roberts settled back in his chair, an amused smile flickering over his face. "So, you're hoping for a bit more excitement. A bit more running around, chasing after bad guys. Like they do in the movies."

There was a dangerous edge to his smile now. "Not necessarily like that. . . ." stammered Shaw.

Roberts's voice dropped to a low hiss. "The SIU cracks cases exactly because we don't work like that. We think, we wait, we anticipate. It's a complex process that a beat cop might find a little beneath him, but we've found it gets results. You understand?"

"Yes, of course, sir. Sorry, sir."

Then, all of a sudden, the malice was gone, and the amusement had returned to Roberts's face. "Anyway, we're meeting someone this afternoon who I think will be able to help us with the case. He may well have some valuable information. And if you're still bored after that, I'll try and do something to liven things up. Shoot someone or something like that. OK? Ah good, here's the food."

After the meal, they lingered over coffee before heading back out into the late afternoon. Their vehicle — a gun-metal gray Mercedes with blacked-out windows — was parked across the street from the restaurant. Shaw had never seen such an expensive car used for police work, but he was getting the feeling that Roberts tended to work according to different rules from other cops.

Shaw climbed into the front seat and rubbed his hands together. "Where are we heading then, sir?"

"Go straight across Waterloo Bridge. I'll direct you from there."

As usual in central London, the traffic was backed up for miles, and the Mercedes inched its way down busy streets. Roberts seemed unconcerned that he might be late for his meeting, and spent the time jotting down notes in a black leather notebook he carried in his inside jacket pocket. Every so often, he would emit a soft chuckle.

Eventually the Mercedes crossed Waterloo Bridge. The sky was now tinged with pink and purple streaks, and although it was still light, the moon was clearly visible. On the south side of the Thames, the London Eye observation wheel rotated slowly, like an exhausted fan. Shaw turned on the radio for company, but a level glare from Roberts made him turn it off again. Could he do anything right with this man?

The Mercedes moved on past Waterloo Station, beyond the grim façades of the buildings on the South Bank. The roads began to change in character, becoming narrower and more winding. Roberts directed Shaw through the maze of backstreets without looking up from his notebook. Eventually they found themselves on a desolate road strewn with trash and plastic bags. On one side a row of lockup garages huddled underneath a bridge, their brickwork black with grime.

"Pull up here," ordered Roberts, his head still buried in the book. He finished his sentence, then slipped the notebook back into his pocket and got out through the passenger door. Shaw made to follow, but the head of the SIU looked around and shook his head. "You stay here and keep an eye on the car. Unattended Mercs don't tend to stay that way very long around here. I'll be back soon."

And with that he slammed the car door shut and strode toward the nearest lockup garage. As Shaw looked on he unlocked the shutters and lifted them up, before disappearing inside. The police officer was fuming. He wanted to be at the meeting, not sitting around here like some kind of night watchman! Not for the first time, he wished that he had never been selected for the SIU.

He had just started to doze off when the roaring sound of an engine made Shaw sit up with surprise. A flaming-red motorbike was careening down the street toward him. At the very last second, it swerved wildly to the right and into the garage that Roberts had just opened up. The bike disappeared as quickly as it had arrived, leaving only a dark drip of oil and a set of tire marks on the surface of the road. Behind it, a plastic bag fluttered forlornly across the pavement.

Shaw hurriedly got out of the car. There was no way he was going to miss this no matter what Roberts said. He turned on the Mercedes's alarm with a beeper and crept to the edge of the garage. Glancing furtively up and down the street, he checked to make sure that no one was watching him. It was empty. He pressed his back to the brickwork and placed his ear as close as he could to the opening. Immediately Shaw recognized the imperious tone of voice that Roberts used when he was telling people off.

". . . and if the Starling boy dies she will regret it. I am *very* unhappy, Silas. When you speak to her, make sure she understands that, won't you?"

"I try . . ."

Shaw shuddered. The man Roberts was speaking to had a cold, reptilian voice with slithering vowels.

". . . I try, but you know Marianne. She doesn't listen to many people."

"She will listen to me. Everyone listens to me." It was said starkly, without a trace of arrogance, and in that moment Shaw could well believe it.

"She is a natural hunter . . . maybe she will not stop. The boy has made the crossing to Darkside, after all. Maybe he has had an accident. Maybe he's dead already. What are you going to do then?"

There was a hint of mockery in the man's voice that only made the sound worse. Goose bumps broke out on Shaw's skin. Where in God's name was that accent from? Shaw couldn't think of any language that hissed like that. Wherever he was from, he didn't sound like the sort of person that Roberts should be dealing with. Shaw remembered the captain saying that there was "something fishy" about the Biloxi case. If he was referring to this person, he was dead right.

"Let's hope that Marianne can recognize a warning when she hears it and takes all the necessary precautions. She will bring the boy to me, or you know what I will do."

The reptilian man hissed with pleasure. "I like to see that fight one day. It might be closer than you think."

There was a loud thud from inside the garage, and Shaw winced. Was Roberts all right in there? With great caution he poked his head around the side of the open shutters and surveyed the scene. The low-ceilinged garage was shabby and cluttered with an array of oily and rusty machine parts. The red motorbike was gleaming on its stand toward the back. By the near wall, Roberts was standing with his back to Shaw. He was holding a wrench in his left hand. His companion was lying on the floor, but Shaw couldn't make out any of his features because Roberts was obscuring his view.

When the head of the SIU spoke again, his voice was icy with anger. "Do you really think that it would be that close?" He leaned down and grabbed the other man by the collar. "You're nothing but a go-between, Silas, a penny-scrabbling messenger boy. How close do you think it would be between me and you?"

There was no reply, only a soft hissing noise.

"I agree. Now get out of here and go give Marianne the good news."

The other man picked himself up off the floor. Shaw suddenly realized that if Roberts found out that he had been eavesdropping, he was in big trouble. As he pulled his head back away from the doorway he caught a glimpse of the reptilian man's face. It was dark and pock-marked and covered with peeling flaps of flesh. The man must have had some sort of horrible skin disease, because he didn't look human. Shaw stood breathing against the side of the wall for a moment as a wave of nausea swept over him. Then there was a scream of an engine from inside the garage, and the red bike flew out into the street. Regaining his composure, Shaw ran back to the Mercedes, his raincoat flapping in the wind. He pressed the beeper frantically, unlocking the car before collapsing in the front seat. A second later, Roberts appeared and closed the garage door. He walked in a businesslike manner back to the car and got in.

With a Herculean effort, Shaw managed to prevent himself from panting as he spoke. "How did the meeting go, sir?"

Roberts granted him a broad grin. "Surprisingly smoothly, Shaw. I haven't lost my powers of persuasion. Hopefully that will have a large impact on the case. Right, then. I could murder a coffee. What about you?"

# 16

Carnegie and Jonathan walked down Savage Row in silence, the rain slanting down through the leafy treetops. The sky was an unforgiving black, and the wind nipped at the tips of ears and fingers like a small angry dog. Inside the huge mansions there would be lamps and roaring fires to ward off the darkness and the cold, but outside there was no escape. In the distance Jonathan could see bolts of lightning crackling over the chimneys and roofs that clustered together around the Grand.

Raindrops dripped down from the brim of Carnegie's hat onto his face. He loped along the road, his hands deep in his pockets. Once he made as if to say something to Jonathan, but bit his lip and turned away again. Feeling thoroughly miserable, Jonathan trailed behind and wished that he was inside. He would have given anything to have been back in his bedroom in London, watching TV in bed, but that seemed like another world. At that moment in time, he would have settled for the sparse comfort of Carnegie's lodgings.

He caught up with the wereman and tapped him on the shoulder. "Look, I'm sorry I've caused you so much trouble. . . ."

Carnegie grimaced. "That's all right, kid. I'm used to trouble. Though even by my standards, this is a lot of trouble."

"It's all my fault. I should never have come here," Jonathan said bitterly.

"Your dad knows what he's doing. If he thought you were safe in Lightside, he wouldn't have sent you over here."

"I don't exactly feel safe here either."

"No," he conceded. "You may have a point there. But don't worry about it. We'll sort out Marianne, and then we'll sort out Vendetta, and then we'll get you back to Alain. Everything will be fine."

Jonathan gave him a dubious look. "You really think so?"

"No. But you've got to be positive about these things. I mean, I was this close to eating you. But you're still here, aren't you?"

"If you get me out of this," Jonathan said mournfully, "you can eat my hand if you want. Vendetta's going to chop it off anyway, so I won't be needing it."

Carnegie barked with laughter and ruffled Jonathan's hair. He reflected that maybe things could be worse, after all.

They continued their slow progress back toward the center of Darkside, and gradually the expensive houses and the trees became obscured behind vast factories and the columns of black smoke churning out from their chimneys. Carnegie led the way through a warren of side streets and alleyways, never faltering or taking a wrong turn. The factory walls were so high and unforgiving that they made Jonathan feel like a rodent in some sort of laboratory experiment. For all the loud clanking of machinery, the explosions of steam, and the ceaseless billowing of smoke, he couldn't see the people who actually worked in the factories. There were no windows in any of the walls, hiding the ranks of Darksiders who toiled away inside.

In one alleyway a pair of young men were leaning idly against the wall. Their muddy, worn clothes barely covered their skeletal limbs. Spotting Jonathan and Carnegie, they stepped out into their path. One of them produced a dirty knife from his pocket and waved it under Carnegie's nose.

"Give us your money," he spat through broken teeth.

The wereman shook his head. "Can't do that, boys."

"Give us your money, or I'll cut you open!"

"Have we not met before? I'm Carnegie."

At the mention of his name, one of the robbers blanched. He tugged his companion's sleeve urgently, and motioned with his eyes to move away. Carnegie watched them back away with benign interest.

"That's right, boys. You've made a very grave error. Shouldn't you be running?"

He bent his head back and unleashed a high-pitched howl that reverberated off the factory walls. As he watched the two robbers flee, Jonathan was reminded of Raquella's words on the Grand: *Everyone knows Carnegie.*

Two streets later, he concluded that thinking about Vendetta's maid only made him even more confused. She had clearly recognized him in the greenhouse. But he had told her that his name was Jonathan. Why hadn't she said anything when he was introduced as someone else? If Vendetta found out that she knew who he was . . . Jonathan thought back to the corpse in the greenhouse and shuddered.

They had been walking for some time now, and the wound in his side was beginning to throb again. He stopped and bent over, holding his side. Carnegie looked on with concern.

"You all right, boy?"

"Yeah. Just a bit tired."

"That wound giving you pain?"

"Little bit. Be all right."

Carnegie's eyes narrowed to slits. "That's very brave of you, son, but we'll get a hansom cab anyway. We're coming out on Princeville Street. We'll be able to get one there."

They came out onto a wider road packed with terraced housing. Carnegie shooed away a couple of small children from a front doorstep and made Jonathan sit down on it. The rain was coming down harder now and bouncing off the cobblestones. The road was clear of carriages, and Jonathan wondered how long they were going to have to wait for a cab to pass. It wasn't as if they could phone for one.

As it turned out, it didn't take that long at all. After a couple of minutes a hansom cab drew smoothly up to the curb.

"Fitzwilliam Street, driver," barked Carnegie.

The driver, immersed in a thick brown cloak and hat against the elements, nodded and gestured at the door. Carnegie helped Jonathan up the steps and into the carriage as the horses stamped their hooves impatiently.

The interior was cramped and dark, but it seemed like paradise to Jonathan. It even smelled familiar somehow. Carnegie followed behind him, hunching over to fit through the door. A woman already occupied one of the seats. She was dressed for mourning, all in black, and a veil was drawn over her face.

"Oh, I'm sorry," began Jonathan. "I didn't realize . . ."

"It's fine," replied the widow. She spoke in a whisper they could barely hear. "I am happy to share the carriage. It is not an evening to be standing waiting in the cold." She paused. "And it is nice to have the company."

Carnegie removed his hat and shook himself

vigorously, sending a spray of water droplets flying across the carriage. "Excuse me," he said, looking entirely unrepentant.

"Good evening, sir. Are you traveling far?"

"Fitzwilliam Street."

"What a pleasant coincidence. So am I."

The widow settled back into her seat, seemingly satisfied. Jonathan rested his head on the door of the carriage, taking comfort from the sound of the raindrops throwing themselves against the window. They were traveling nearer to the heart of the storm, and thunder rumbled continuously above their heads, as if the black sky were tearing apart at the seams. Every now and again, a flash of lightning would sear his vision, bathing the carriage in a brilliant white light.

Despite the loud frenzy of the weather, the combination of his painful wound and the long walk had made Jonathan feel very tired. He was just about to drift off to sleep when the widow opposite adjusted her bonnet. A single shining white hair dropped into her lap, stark against the black folds of her dress. As the thunderclouds unleashed another monumental roar, a wave of fear swept over Jonathan.

"Carnegie!" he screamed. "It's Marianne!"

Beside him, the wereman had slumped into a daze, overcome by the effects of her sleeping scent. Marianne chuckled and lifted up her veil, revealing her pale skin.

"Hello, Jonathan. You didn't think we'd forget about you, did you?" She drew a slender dagger from her boot. Carnegie slapped himself around the face, trying to clear his head. Marianne laughed again. "You both look tired. Why don't you go back to sleep?"

Carnegie lunged toward her, but his energy had been sapped. The raging beast that had attacked Jonathan was nowhere to be seen, and in his place was a large, tired man. His lumbering movements contrasted with Marianne's speed and sharpness. She flashed her dagger at him, slicing him across the arm. The wereman yelled with pain. He aimed a blow with his other fist, but missed Marianne completely. Instead his fist shattered the near window, and rain and cold air flooded into the carriage.

Jonathan felt the cobwebs begin to clear from his head, and realized that had been Carnegie's plan. The wereman was down on the floor of the carriage, blood pouring from his arms. Marianne swore and made to stab him in the back, but Jonathan snaked out a leg and kicked the dagger from her hand.

Up on the roof of the cab, the driver began to lash his horses mercilessly, urging them to go faster and faster. The carriage hurtled onward into the night, rocking from side to side like a boat in a storm. Inside, it was nearly impossible for anyone to stand up. As Marianne scrabbled around for her dagger the driver took a sudden right turn, sending all three occupants crashing into the door. For a second Jonathan could feel Carnegie's bulk slumped against him, and hear Marianne's breath close by his ear, before the carriage righted itself and the three of them fell back to the floor.

Carnegie groaned and tried to push himself up, only to receive a swift knee in the ribs from Marianne. He collapsed again. Clearly, the wereman was having trouble shaking off the effects of the bounty hunter's scent. Jonathan dived for the dagger, curling his fingers around the hilt. Marianne went after him, trying to prize the weapon free with her nails. As they tumbled around Jonathan became aware of a loud scratching noise coming from the roof of the carriage. He glanced up and, with a sinking heart, saw Skeet's sharp, bald head poking down from the top of the window. Unaffected by the breakneck speed of the carriage, the creature swung down from the luggage rail and rested his feet on the ledge by the door so that he was pressed flat against the side of the vehicle.

"Carnegie! Wake up! Skeet's coming!"

There was an angry snarl in response, and suddenly Jonathan felt Marianne being hoisted off him. The wereman tossed her into a heap on top of the seat and turned back to face the other threat. He was just in time. Having yanked open the door, Skeet was already inside the carriage. He went straight for Carnegie, fingers aiming for his eyes. The detective wrapped his arms around him and wrestled him to the floor. In the melee Marianne caught a stray boot to the chin, sending her sprawling across the carriage. Behind her head, the door banged excitedly open and shut.

The bounty hunter lodged herself in a corner and screamed, "Humble!" at the top of her voice. At the signal the driver made another devilish right turn, lurching the carriage over onto two wheels. Jonathan took a painful tumble into the corner of a seat, the impact jarring Marianne's dagger from his hand. Carnegie and Skeet slid across the floor, still grappling, and heading inexorably toward the open door.

"Noooo!" Jonathan cried.

It was too late. The two creatures rolled over once more, and then dropped out of the side of the carriage, hitting the road with a loud crash. Marianne whooped with triumph and banged on the roof. The carriage fell down onto all four wheels again, and began to slow to a normal trot. She carefully rearranged her ruffled widow costume, reclaimed her dagger, and shut the door. The blade gleamed menacingly in her hand. Marianne smiled.

"I think that should do it. Well now, little one, shall we go and see William Grimshaw? He's been just dying to meet you."

# 17

The carriage flew on like a bat through the maze of backstreets. This part of Darkside reeked of poverty. The streets were dank and strewn with trash, the houses on the point of collapse. On the sidewalks, young children huddled around small fires, their ragged clothing struggling to stay on their thin limbs. They looked up as the coach went past, and cast envious glances inside it.

At that moment, despite the cold and the rain, Jonathan would have happily switched places with them. He sat on his hands, trying to think. Marianne had placed her dagger down on the seat next to her, and withdrawn a small compact from the folds of her dress. Now she dabbed at her face with powder.

"I really should think about doing something different," she mused. "All this fighting is wreaking havoc on my complexion. If only it didn't pay so well. . . ."

Jonathan remained silent.

"What is it, little one? Are you upset with me?"

"I want to go home," Jonathan said stubbornly. "Let me out of here!"

"I almost wish that I could. But you're much too valuable to let go, little one." She leaned in closer to him, and stroked a finger across his cheek. The familiar scent of her perfume drifted back under Jonathan's nostrils. "You might be angry with me now, but you'll forgive me. Because I know how unique and special you are. Has anyone ever told you how unique and special you are?"

He shook his head slowly, unwilling to catch her eye.

"Well, I am now. And Grimshaw thinks you are too. He just has a different way of expressing it. Oh, good! Here we are!"

The carriage had turned up a devastated street, where the houses had collapsed into dazed piles of rubble. There were no signs of life among the ruins. And then, in the middle of the wasteland, Jonathan caught sight of a dilapidated concert hall, with a small railed courtyard protecting it from the harsh outside world. As the carriage drew nearer, it was possible to see a crowd of Darksiders milling in the courtyard outside. They were dressed in somber-colored suits and long dresses, but their eyes were wild as if they were on drugs. Ten-foot braziers blazed with flames that twisted and danced over their heads.

In the driver's seat Humble reined in the horses, and the carriage came to a complete stop. Jonathan stayed frozen in his chair, suddenly afraid of stepping outside. The front doors to the hall were closed and studded with iron bands. On either side a squat plinth bore a creature carved from marble: to the left, a leopard, and to the right, a rhinoceros. A banner had been draped above the entrance, which read WILLIAM GRIMSHAW'S WORLD FAMOUS BEASTILIA EXOTICA! Tattered posters had been pasted onto the walls, boasting lurid paintings of snakes, lions, and spiders. Every animal had its jaws open, as if it were ready to strike. From somewhere, Jonathan could hear the faint strains of mournful classical music drifting up to his ears.

The giant mute, still wrapped in the thick, long coachman's coat, opened the carriage door and pulled

Jonathan out of the carriage. Marianne descended daintily after him, lifting the hem of her dress away from the wet cobbles.

"Thank you, Humble. That was some rather amazing driving back there."

The mute bowed his head in reply. He made a signal to Marianne with his hands. She wrinkled her nose. "Skeet? He rolled off the carriage a few minutes back. He knows where to find us. If Carnegie hasn't killed him first, of course."

Humble and Marianne positioned themselves on either side of Jonathan.

"Don't try and run off again, little one."

"I'll scream for help," Jonathan threatened fiercely.

Marianne cackled. "Look around you, dear. You're in Darkside. Who do you think is going to help you here?"

In the midst of the crowd a bald, elderly man with a monocle turned around to stare at the new arrivals. Jonathan gave him a pleading look that shouted out *Help me!* The man bared his teeth in response. They had all been filed down to sharp points. Jonathan shrank back in horror, and moved closer to Marianne.

"I thought you might see it my way. Is it nearly

time yet? I'm not standing in the rain all night while Grimshaw decides when to open up."

Humble gave her a sympathetic glance, and draped his enormous coat over her shoulders. She patted his hand in thanks. The classical music was growing in volume, and beneath the yearning strings there was a rumble of percussion that Jonathan felt in the depths of his belly. A murmur of expectation ran through the crowd. The music got louder and louder, ringing around the deserted street and exploding like fireworks into the Darkside night. Then, without warning, the music stopped, and the front doors swung mysteriously inward. The crowd began to shuffle inside.

Marianne sighed. "I think Grimshaw's getting too melodramatic for his own good." Struck by a sudden thought, she turned to Jonathan. "Stay close to me, little one. There can be some nasty things inside the Exotica, and I haven't spent all this time hunting you down only to lose you now."

They were the last of the crowd to head up the stairs, and make their way down a curving hallway. Dirty red lightbulbs cast a sullen glow over the darkness. Glass-fronted cabinets had been built into the walls, where scraggly animals sat glumly. As Jonathan walked past one, a chimpanzee leaped forward and banged furiously on the windowpane, making him jump.

"Are you sure we're safe here?" he hissed at Marianne.

"Not really. That's the point of the Exotica. The animals are allowed to get very close to you. You see, you don't pay to get *in*. You pay to get *out*. That's a very important difference."

"I don't understand."

"It's probably best for you that you don't, little one."

She squeezed his hand, and again Jonathan found himself confused by his kidnapper's capacity to show him kindness. He knew that she was dangerous and that he should hate her, but he just couldn't. In a strange way, at that exact moment in time, he was glad she was there.

The hallway continued to wind around in a leisurely circle. Jonathan stuck close to Marianne and Humble, and took great care not to go too close to the display cases. It was like no zoo he had ever been near before. There were no signs by the windows, so he was often unsure of what was inside. But he could hear the creatures rustling, could see shapes scuttling away to the safety of the dark corners. There was a lingering threat in the air that made everyone quiet and tense. Even Humble appeared to be affected, his strange near-permanent smile replaced by a watchful look.

They had dropped back far behind the rest of the visitors, and when the silence was shattered by a yell of surprise, it came from far ahead. Instinctively Humble and Marianne shielded Jonathan. Suddenly the old gentleman with the filed-down teeth came back around the corner, staggering like a drunk and clutching his throat. It took Jonathan a moment to make out the snake wrapped around his neck like a noose, its scales gleaming in the bloodred light. He gasped as it casually, almost lazily, tightened its grip, sending the man crashing to his knees. He scrabbled desperately for another breath, but it never came, and in a matter of seconds he had fallen to the floor, dead.

Marianne looked on impassively. "Grimshaw's been removing the windows from the display cases again," she said. "We really need to keep an eye out."

"Shouldn't we have done something?" Jonathan asked, fixated by the scene in front of him.

"Like what? He was dead the second he went too close to that snake. Now, for goodness sake, mind your step."

Without a second glance, she skirted around the prone figure of the old man. His face had turned blue, and there was a look of shock etched onto it. The snake lay coiled around him, unmoved by all the commotion except for the vicious, hungry flicking of its tongue into the air. Jonathan met its unblinking gaze and edged carefully around it.

After several nervous minutes the hallway came out into a large circular room that lay at the heart of the Beastilia Exotica. Banks of seats led down to a lowered stage area in the center of the room. In a balcony overlooking the stage, a conductor was leading an orchestra through a mournful lament. The members of the audience who had survived the walk down the red hallway were now dotted around the room. They waited in complete silence, focusing on the empty scene in front of them.

"What are they waiting for?"

"The main show. That's when the really dangerous animals are allowed out. We don't want to be around for that. Come on. We're going backstage."

Marianne and Humble walked down an aisle between two rows of seats, and made for a side door in the wall to the left of the stage. A hand-painted sign bellowed EXTREME DANGER! PROFESSIONALS ONLY! KEEP OUT! The warning seemed a little unnecessary to Jonathan, given that extreme danger seemed to lurk everywhere in the Beastilia Exotica. Nevertheless, he followed his captors through the door.

They had entered a high-ceilinged hall that bustled with activity and shook with the squawks and growls of a menagerie of animals. There were cages as far as the eye could see: on the floor, piled on top of one another, even hanging from the ceiling. Each one was a tiny prison for a rare animal. In front of Jonathan a rangy cheetah paced with frustration up and down his cage, patchy fur hanging from his haunches. To his immediate left, a black widow spider hung menacingly from the roof of her confinement, while at the top of a stack of birdcages a proud bird of paradise sang songs of fresh air and freedom. Assistants in long brown overalls hurried between the cages, dodging the mounds of fur and feathers that covered the floor. The room stank of fear and desperation.

In the far corner, a man was standing on a wooden walkway that ran around the top of a square glass aquarium. He was tossing chunks of meat from a bucket into the water, causing a frenetic activity among the aquarium's invisible occupants. Fine lines of blood trailed in their wake.

"Grimshaw!"

The man put the bucket down and waited for Marianne and her companions to clamber up the steps to the top of the walkway. As Jonathan approached, he could just make out the slim, dark shapes cutting through the water and a sign gleefully advertising GRIMSHAW'S POOL OF PAIN. Jonathan gripped on to the support rail and stayed well away from the edge. For the first time in a while, the thought of trying to escape reentered his head. Humble was paying close attention to him, however, and it seemed that being alone in the Beastilia Exotica was probably more dangerous than here. For the time being, at least.

"Ah. Marianne, my sweet." Grimshaw bowed, and kissed her hand with a theatrical flourish. He was dressed like a circus ringmaster, in a red top hat and tails. A whip hung from his side. But it was his face that transfixed Jonathan: the crepe-paper skin that showed every gnarl and crevice in his skull, and the different-colored eyes, one green and one blue.

"You are too kind." She crouched down and stared into the water. "What have you got in there? Piranhas?"

"No. The audience got bored of piranhas. There are only so many times you can show them stripping the flesh from a human. I managed to acquire some barracudas instead."

Marianne wrinkled her nose. "Barracudas?"

"They're a spectacularly nasty species of fish. I have high hopes for them."

"I preferred the piranhas. Anyway, I have the boy."

"So I see." He cast his eyes over Jonathan, each pupil moving with total independence from the other. "You are the one who's been causing all the problems? You'd better be worth it."

"What do you want with me?" asked Jonathan nervously.

The green eye narrowed. "Don't you know what you are, boy? You're a crossbreed. Half-Darksider, half-Lightsider. Personally, I prefer thoroughbreds, but you do have a certain . . . freak-show appeal to some of my less discerning customers. So you will take the stage at the Beastilia Exotica. For one night only. With a pack of jackals."

"What am I supposed to do there?"

Grimshaw leaned in close to Jonathan. "You're supposed to die."

"You're insane! This is all crazy! I'm not getting on any stupid stage! Let me out of here!"

Grimshaw exhaled slowly, a horrid slithering sound. "Life can be very cruel sometimes. And so can I. You will perform like a natural, believe me."

Jonathan said nothing. Marianne ruffled his hair affectionately. "Look after him, Grimshaw. He's a good boy. In great demand too. It turns out that you're not the only one who's after him. You're lucky I'm a woman of my word."

"Your honorable reputation precedes you, my dear."

"I should really charge you more for him, but never mind. Speaking of payment, I think you owe me some money. And perhaps an apology for doubting me?"

"Apology? I never doubted you for a second."

From the main hall there was a deafening roar of a wild animal, and a howl of terror. Grimshaw nodded expectantly. "Sounds like the show has begun. There's death in the air."

He picked up the bucket and threw another hunk of meat into the aquarium. The water churned as the barracudas flocked to the surface to feast upon the flesh. The screams continued to carry from the main hall.

Jonathan gulped. "What's happening out there?"

The ringmaster of the Beastilia Exotica scratched his head. "Difficult to say for sure. We sent out an African lion and a snow leopard tonight. Neither of them has been fed for a few days. They might be fighting each other. Or trying to eat the audience. Sounds to me like it's the second one."

A ferocious roar ripped through the air.

"Yes. Definitely the second one."

"Aren't you going to stop it?" gasped Jonathan.

"Stop it? Why would I want to do that? That's the reason people come here! What are they supposed to do otherwise? Just stare at the animals?"

"But people are going to die out there!"

Grimshaw put his hands out in a gesture of helplessness. "The doors open again in twenty minutes. They can leave then. Provided they pay the exit fee, of course."

"But that's crazy! Why do people come here?"

He bent down until his blue eye was on the same level as Jonathan's. "Because it's life. It's tough and it's cruel and it doesn't stop any time you ask it to. Darksiders know that. And if there's one thing they love, it's a good, unfair fight. They'll always come here."

Marianne flung a bored glance around the room. "Grimshaw, the boy's from Lightside. He's not going to appreciate your style of entertainment. It's getting late. Are you going to pay me now?"

"Naturally. Step into my office. The boy is safe with the mute?"

"Humble — make sure the little one doesn't disappear again. If he tries anything funny, put him in the cage like the other one."

The giant nodded and clamped a hand around Jonathan's arm. Grimshaw and Marianne walked behind an enclosure dominated by a baby elephant, and disappeared from sight through an exit. Jonathan thought quickly. He had maybe five minutes until they returned: This was his last chance. He craned his neck up to catch the giant's eye.

"Hi there."

Humble gazed blankly down at him.

"I know that Marianne must pay you loads of money for doing this sort of thing, but my dad would be really pleased to see me again. I bet he'd pay you more if you returned me. Why don't we go and see him and find out?"

A slow smile dawned on Humble's face, and he cuffed Jonathan around the head. It may have been meant as a playful gesture, but the impact made him stagger and bells rang inside his head.

"I'll take that as a no, then."

Humble pointed at the empty cage hanging from the ceiling, and then put a warning finger across his lips. There was no other thing for it. Jonathan was going to have to try to attack the giant. He knew it sounded insane, but maybe he would get lucky. After all, he still had the knife from Alain's ward in his pocket. Maybe Humble would slip and fall in the water. Maybe he would trip and bang his head on the rail, knocking him unconscious. Anything could happen. . . .

Jonathan was considering whether to go for Humble's legs or his arms when a heavy weight came crashing down onto the mute, sending them both tumbling into the depths of the Pool of Pain.

# 18

The aquarium had been wheeled backstage some-time during the day. Ricky was dozing, but the thunderous rolling of the structure and the squealing protests of the wheels woke him up. Grimshaw's assistants swarmed over it like brown-overalled larvae, heaving and pushing it through the labyrinth of cages. Despite their efforts, it seemed hard to believe that it was possible to move the Pool of Pain. Water lapped over the sides as the assistants maneuvered it into the corner of the room directly beneath his cage.

If anything, Ricky was more unnerved by the aquarium beneath him than he had been by the hard stone floor. He had heard the shouts and screams from the main hall the night before, and he knew that the black shapes shifting ceaselessly beneath the surface had been responsible. Feeding time was worst of all. Even from thirty feet in the air, the thrashing and the foaming, and the spreading ink-blots of blood on the water, were a terrible sight. And Ricky couldn't help but notice that Grimshaw was always on hand to feed the fish, doling out scoops of meat from his bucket. He hummed happily to himself as carnage filled the pool.

Ricky tried to spend most of his time asleep, as if he might somehow wake up back in his bedroom at home, with a bottle of Coke, a bag of chips, and a new comic book sitting on his bedside table. It never happened, of course. He spent his time awake staring listlessly out over the hall, with only the hollers and squawks of the animals for company. Some of the chimps waved and stared dolefully back at him, as if they understood how he felt.

Then Marianne and the giant returned, and everything changed. Ricky gaped through the bars with fear when he saw the skinny brown-haired boy being frog-marched between them. He knew who that had to be. The party made their way up to the walkway surrounding the aquarium, and positioned themselves directly beneath his cage.

Whoever the new boy was, he was brave. He stood up straight and looked directly into Grimshaw's terrible eyes, in a way that Ricky could never have dreamed of doing. When Marianne and Grimshaw left the room, he had said something to the giant that earned him a shuddering cuff. It was then that Ricky realized that he had to do something, or they were all dead.

He couldn't explain what made him take off his jacket and begin to wriggle his way through the bars of his cage. The blood was racing through his veins, and his heart felt like it was going to burst, but his head was strangely clear. He inched out between the bars, and swung his feet around to the narrow ledge on the outside of the cage. It wasn't that difficult. A detached voice inside his head guessed that because the cage was so high up, they hadn't worried about the gap between the bars being wider than those that imprisoned the animals on the floor.

The shifting of his weight had made the cage sway from side to side. Ricky could feel the air brushing his face. The mute was directly below him — but such a long way down. A splinter of doubt entered his mind for the first time. This was crazy. There was no way he could be sure he'd survive the fall. Ricky was thinking about slipping between the bars and back into the cage when a howler monkey on the ground, seeing the funny human swinging through the air, pointed up at the ceiling and screamed with amusement. Humble began to tilt his head upward. Everything became very simple then. Ricky screwed his eyes tightly shut and jumped into the air.

The sheer time it took to drop surprised him. It must have lasted only a few seconds, but it felt much longer than that. As the world whizzed past his ears, Ricky could feel momentum building, could feel himself getting heavier and heavier. There was no fear anymore, no pleasure either. He thought that he could have kept on dropping forever, like falling off the side of the world. Then, brutally, he crashed into Humble, and everything went black.

At first the shock of the cold water was the only thing that Jonathan's system could register. His instinct for survival taking over, he kicked for the surface, breaking the waves with a splutter. He wiped the wet hair out of his eyes and surveyed the scene. He had fallen close to the side of the pool, within easy reach of the walkway. Humble was nowhere to be seen, but there was a boy in the water near the far end of the pool. He wasn't moving.

With a shiver of horror, Jonathan remembered the barracudas. He had to get out of there. Frantically scanning the water, he saw a dark shape cutting through the water toward him at high speed. Jonathan launched himself into a front crawl and made for the side of the pool. He was a good swimmer, and he only had a small distance to cover, but the barracuda was designed for underwater pursuit, and as Jonathan hauled himself out of the water, it managed to close the gap and fasten its jaws around his foot. He shouted with pain, and hung onto the walkway rail to avoid being dragged back into the pool. Twisting his body around, he managed to smash his other foot onto the barracuda's head, which was protruding above the surface. His kick connected well enough to make it release its grip, and the fish slunk back into the depths.

Jonathan dragged himself onto the walkway and away from the edge of the water. That had been too close. His sneaker had been cut to shreds in the attack, and his ankle was bleeding badly. A sudden flash of silver in the water caught his eye, and he realized that, in the mad dash for safety, his knife had slipped from his pocket and was now sinking to the bottom of the pool. His only weapon in this nightmare was gone. For one crazy second Jonathan thought about diving in to retrieve it, but he managed to stop himself in time. There were more important things to think about. The other boy was still lying in the water, and the barracudas were beginning to circle around him. Jonathan had no idea what to do. There was no way that he could jump in and save him — they would both be dead meat. He looked around for some kind of pole to drag him to safety, but there was nothing of the sort on hand. The barracudas were nearing their target. He couldn't watch.

With a massive whoosh Humble broke the surface of the Pool of Pain, his long arms flailing desperately. A mini tidal wave surged away from his body and crashed into the walkway. The giant was having problems keeping himself afloat, and his head kept disappearing back under the water. His flailing movements immediately caught the attention of the barracudas, and they made a beeline for him.

Jonathan realized that this was his chance. He hobbled around the side of the pool, leaning his weight on his good ankle. The first barracuda darted in at Humble, who tried to shift out of the way. He didn't move quickly enough, and as the fish snapped at his fingers he opened his mouth and let out a silent cry of pain. The power and speed that he had displayed on dry land was gone now. He was vulnerable, and the barracudas knew it.

Trying not to attract any attention, Jonathan lowered himself slowly into the water. He stroked smoothly toward the boy, his ankle throbbing in protest at the exertion. The water was choppy with the battle between Humble and the barracudas. Foam flicked up into his eyes as he swam. He reached the boy, who stirred slightly as Jonathan put an arm around his neck in a lifesaving hold, and began to drag him back to the side.

The onslaught of the barracudas against Humble continued mercilessly. The mute giant struggled on, blood seeping out from a series of wounds. Occasionally his hands would fasten onto one of the fish, and he would wring the life out of it. But they kept on coming, and he was running out of energy.

On the other side of the pool, it was slow going, and Jonathan had to rely on his legs to propel them both. As he kicked out he saw the trail of blood dripping from his ankle, and knew that they were in trouble. Sensing the blood in the water, one of the barracudas turned and arrowed after it. Jonathan redoubled his efforts, but the boy he was dragging was heavy and they were still far from the walkway.

"Wake up!" he shouted in the boy's ear. "You've got to wake up!"

The boy's eyelids fluttered in response. He would probably come around just in time to be devoured. Jonathan took a quick glance at the side. They were eight or nine strokes away. Another barracuda had separated itself from the main pack and was making for them.

"WAKE UP!"

The boy's eyes flicked open, and he began coughing.

"Swim!" Jonathan shouted again. "Swim to the side! Hurry!"

Reacting as if on autopilot, the boy began paddling. Freed from his deadweight, Jonathan made powerfully for the edge of the pool. Behind him, the fish were moving at terrifying speed, their sleek bodies bisecting the waves. Drawing on his last reserves of strength he pulled himself out of the pool for the second time, and looked for the other boy.

Despite his confusion, the boy was nearing safety. Jonathan stretched out an arm and shouted at him, "Come on! They're gaining on you!"

The boy moaned and tried to paddle faster. As the first barracuda zeroed in on his leg, he made one last surge through the water. Jonathan's fingers latched onto his arm and yanked him up toward the walkway. The sudden movement took the barracuda by surprise, and its swoop missed the intended target. The boy scrabbled up and onto the walkway and lay coughing and spitting water.

Jonathan hauled him up by the arms. "We have to get out of here," he urged. "They'll be back in a minute."

The boy nodded, and staggered to his feet. Bruised, battered, and bleeding, the pair of them hobbled off the top of the walkway and back down among the cages. In the water, the surviving barracudas attacked the giant with renewed vigor.

From the other side of the hall there was a huge uproar, and Jonathan pressed the boy against the side of an antelope's cage. Marianne raced past. "Humble!" she screamed. "Hold on! I'm coming!"

She raced up the steps and dived into the Pool of Pain, her brilliant white hair flashing like a shooting star. Jonathan glanced left and right, and made for a door on the left-hand wall. The boy tugged his sleeve and pointed at the cages around them.

"The . . . animals," he panted. "We shouldn't . . . leave them."

Jonathan shook his head. "There's no time. We've got to get out of here."

He dragged the boy through the door, and they found themselves back in the curving red hallway. It was deathly quiet now; only the faintest of muffled shouts could be heard from the main hall. There was no one in sight. A cabinet in front of them was empty, and there were shards of glass sprinkled on the floor. Jonathan leaned against the wall, and as he caught his breath, exchanged names with Ricky.

"Thanks for that. That was some jump. You could have killed yourself!"

Ricky looked abashed. "Guess so. It looked like we were both dead anyway, so I didn't really think about it." He paused, looking around. "This place is horrible. Where *are* we?"

"I'll tell you all about it when we get out of here. You aren't going to believe it, though."

Suddenly a hulking shape emerged from the gloom in front of them. Ricky let out a bloodcurdling scream.

# 19

Mrs. Elwood folded her arms obstinately. "If you're going to treat me like a criminal, then I'm going to wait for my lawyer. You're not going to get another word out of me."

Officer Shaw resisted the urge to put his head in his hands. Things were not going as smoothly as he had hoped. Though Roberts kept saying there wasn't anything specific to link the two cases, Shaw was convinced that the disappearance of the Starling boy was connected to the Thomas kidnapping. There was something about the method of attack — flamboyant and daring, in full view of other people. In both cases, there should have been a stream of witnesses, but there were none. So when Shaw had heard that a woman had given a statement concerning the Starling affair, he wondered if this was going to be the breakthrough that would solve the case. Instinctively he thought of giving a victorious statement to the media announcing the rescue of the two boys and bathing in the warmth of their applause.

Then he had met Mrs. Elwood, and all his triumphant daydreams vanished. From the very first second of their meeting in the police station, his one prospective witness had proved belligerent and uncooperative. She had objected to going to the interview room, complained about the cup of coffee he had brought her, and was now refusing to give a coherent statement.

He tried again. "I'm not treating you like a criminal, ma'am. I just wanted to go over your statement again. I know you must have been upset that day — you went through a very traumatic experience. Now that you've had a day or so to calm down, you might remember things a bit differently."

"You want me to change my statement?"

"I'd like you to confirm that some of the details you gave us are correct, that's all."

"Like what, exactly?"

Officer Shaw sighed and began to read out her

statement. " 'Then a giant man, around seven feet in height, began to attack the car. He pulled the front passenger door off its hinges with his bare hands. Jonathan scrambled to the backseat and escaped on the other side of the car. The giant dropped the door and set off in pursuit after him.' Surely you can understand why someone might find it hard to believe that you were attacked in the middle of London by a giant who was able to rip your car door off with his hands?"

Mrs. Elwood's eyes narrowed dangerously. "You'd better not be calling me a liar, young man. We were surrounded by people at the time. There must be some witnesses. Have you seen my car? How do you think that happened? Did I do it myself?"

"Unfortunately, ma'am, no one has come forward to support your story. Sometimes people can be reluctant to come forward as witnesses. We've interviewed a handful of people, but all of them claimed that they didn't see anything. We haven't given up hope yet, though."

"I should think not. Instead of interrogating me, you should be out looking for Jonathan. Anything could have happened to him. What am I supposed to say to his father?"

Officer Shaw tried to inject a soothing tone into his voice. "We have a squad of officers out combing the area for him now. Initially we're focusing on the Thames Path on the north side of the river. If there are any clues as to Jonathan's current whereabouts, we'll find them there."

Mrs. Elwood harrumphed, unconvinced. Shaw sighed. "Well, I suppose that's it for now. We'll need to speak to you again at some point, but it's late. I understand that Jonathan's father is unwell?"

She nodded. "He doesn't really know what's going on around him. . . ." Her voice trailed off. "It might be for the best, what with Jonathan . . ."

Officer Shaw handed her a card with his phone number on it. "You should take this. If you think of anything else about that night, anything at all, then call me and let me know."

Again she nodded, and Shaw excused himself from the interview. The woman was clearly shaken up by what had happened to her. That could be the only explanation for her batty statement. He hoped that she would come around and give him something in the realm of reality to go on. At the moment, the investigation was stumbling down a series of dead ends, and everyone was starting to feel the pressure.

The situation was not helped by the fact that Carter Roberts had vanished. Shaw had come into work to find a terse message on his voice mail, informing him that Roberts had gone up north to follow a lead. Since then he had heard nothing more from him, save for one rather unsatisfactory conversation on the phone. The line was crackly, and it was difficult for each man to hear the other.

"Is that you, Shaw?"

"Sorry?"

"IS THAT YOU, SHAW?" Roberts bellowed.

"Oh. Yes, sir. Sorry, sir."

"Has there been any more news about the Starling boy?"

"No, sir. We've got that crazy woman coming in again to go over her statement. Hopefully she'll give us something a bit more useful than giants with superhuman strength."

He snickered, but his boss seemed less amused. "Shut up, Shaw. You can make stupid jokes when you've retrieved Starling. Is there anything else?"

"Might be one other thing. I've just talked to Ricky Thomas's mom. She thinks the boy was getting picked on at school. I was just wondering, sir — maybe he wasn't kidnapped at all. Maybe he just ran away."

Roberts gave a disinterested grunt. "Forget about the Thomas boy for now. He's not the key to the case. Concentrate on finding Starling."

"Well, we're trying, sir, but it's not that simple. We've got a team out looking for him, but he seems to have vanished off the face of the earth."

There was a pause.

"Look harder," said Roberts, and abruptly put the phone down.

Shaw was still seething about it now, as he paced through the long corridors of the police station. It had felt like they were getting close to something, but now it was back to square one. He was heading back to reception when a young out-of-breath deputy caught up with him.

"Shaw! Wait!"

"What is it?"

"You've got to come and have a look at something. You're not going to believe it, but you should have a look anyway."

He led him up to a surveillance room on the second floor. Inside it was dark, the only light provided by a bank of television screens. The deputy seemed a little unsure of himself, and launched into a rapid explanation.

"When I saw it, I thought it had to be some sort of technical glitch or something like that, but I talked to some of our tech guys and they said that there's nothing wrong with the tape so it must be sort of real. I guess."

Officer Shaw scratched his head impatiently. "I have no idea what you're talking about."

The deputy hit the play button on a VCR. A fuzzy black-and-white picture emerged on the screen, showing an empty street. "We got some surveillance video from a camera down by the Thames Path near Blackfriars. See?"

On the screen, a small figure came racing along the path, his legs pumping at high speed.

"That must be the Starling boy," breathed Shaw. "Where exactly is this camera? We need men down there now!"

"That's not all. . . . Watch."

The screen flickered, and then a blur of motion flew down the center of the path.

"What the heck was that?"

The policeman wound the tape back in slow motion. Gradually, the motion blur revealed itself to be a man. But, judging by the time in the bottom right corner of the video footage, he had covered the ground beneath the camera at an impossible speed. Shaw couldn't believe his eyes.

"That can't be a person! No one can run that fast!"

"I know. And have you seen how tall he is?"

Officer Shaw sucked in his breath. At a rough guess, the elongated figure had to be around seven feet. The batty old woman had been right. Something was going on here that Shaw didn't quite understand, but it was becoming increasingly clear that this case was bigger and stranger than he could ever have imagined. After all, this wasn't the first time this week that he had seen an otherworldly creature on the streets of London. One thing was clear: He needed to find Roberts, and fast.

# 20

"If you don't shut your friend up, I'm going to do it for you."

Jonathan's first response at seeing Carnegie was to yell with relief, but the sound died in his throat. Carnegie's voice was low and thick, and an animal rasping noise emanated from his lungs. The private detective had mutated into the beast again. Even in the dim red light Jonathan could tell that the wereman had been in a fierce struggle. His clothes were torn to shreds, and there was a long slash running down the side of his cheek. The thick gray hair on his face was matted with blood. Only the hat perched on his head provided any link to Carnegie the human.

Beside Jonathan, Ricky was now mute with horror. Jonathan tugged his trembling shirtsleeve. "It's all right. I know this guy. He's a friend."

Carnegie ran the back of his hand across his mouth and stared at the two boys. His eyes were bleary and unfocused. "What's your name, son?"

"R–R–Ricky."

"You look lost, boy."

"I was kidnapped," he said, hesitantly. "I was on a school trip and then . . . Marianne . . . and now I don't know where I am."

Carnegie nodded slowly. "Better off that way," he growled.

"I'm sorry?"

"Doesn't matter. Follow me."

The wereman turned and headed off down the hallway. He was limping badly.

"Are you all right?" Jonathan asked him nervously.

"Fine. Never better."

"How did you know where to find us?"

"I had a word in Skeet's ear. I persuaded him to tell me everything."

"What did you do to him?"

Carnegie's face's twisted into a snarl. "Enough questions."

"Oh. OK. Sorry."

They walked cautiously on through the murky passage, broken glass crunching beneath their feet. Jonathan kept a lookout for any more wild beasts, but it appeared that they had been driven by the same impulse to escape as everyone else, and nothing lurked in wait for them.

They were nearing the exit when the classical music that had heralded their entrance began booming once more, shattering the silence and making Ricky jump violently. The music was being played so loudly that every discordant screech of a violin string sent a nerve throbbing in Jonathan's forehead.

"Show's over!" Carnegie shouted above the racket. "Grimshaw's opening the front door."

"For who? Everyone's dead!"

"We're still here, aren't we?"

They rounded another corner and saw the exit to the Beastilia Exotica standing wide open. To Jonathan, the Darkside night looked appealing in a way it never had before. He couldn't stand to be in the ghastly red hallway for one second longer. Both he and Ricky began walking more quickly, overtaking Carnegie as they hurried to get outside.

They trotted out into the nighttime courtyard, breathing a sigh of relief as they passed through the doors and out of the house of horrors. The braziers were burning down, and the moon was low in the sky. Ricky smiled and turned to say something to Jonathan but then stopped, and the grin faded from his face. From out of the shadows by the main gate William Grimshaw stepped forward, the torchlight dancing in his discolored eyes. His whip was uncurled and twitched angrily in his hand like a snake.

"Leaving so soon, boys? You didn't even get to see the show."

Jonathan glanced nervously back to the doorway just as Carnegie hauled himself through it. When Grimshaw saw him a look of surprise crossed his face.

"Carnegie! What are you doing here?"

The wereman nodded at the boys. "Came for these two. Have you got a problem with that?"

"I have, actually. It's cost me a great deal of time

and money to get my hands on these young humans, and now it seems that people are trying to double-cross me."

"Life's hard. Now get out of my way."

"Carnegie, you're meddling in an important business transaction. What are the mongrels to you, anyway?"

"That's my business. We're leaving."

"I don't have any argument with you. Maybe we could come to some sort of . . . financial agreement?"

Carnegie had had enough. He howled and lunged at Grimshaw. Startled, the ringmaster took aim with his whip, but he was too late. The wereman caught him by the arm and ripped the weapon from his hand, hurling it across the courtyard. Then he raised a hand and struck Grimshaw across the face with a savage blow. The man crumpled beneath the force of the strike, falling to his knees. Carnegie raised his hand again.

"No!" screamed Jonathan.

The wereman turned, his face beastlike.

"Don't do it! You'll kill him!"

"And?"

There was a dangerous edge to his voice. Jonathan

realized that he was no longer talking to a private detective, but standing between an animal and its prey. "You don't need to kill him. Look at him!"

Grimshaw hung like a puppet from Carnegie's grip, his eyes glazed over and his legs trailing uselessly across the ground.

"You're a long way from home, boy. Maybe you should keep your mouth shut."

"He's not worth it." Jonathan tried to keep his voice low and firm and free from any trace of fear. "If you kill him, you'll be no better than he is."

Carnegie snarled and raised his hand again. "I'll kill what and who I want. Get in my way, boy, and you'll find that out the hard way. Bullet or no bullet."

"That's not you talking. I know you. You're more than just a killer."

Jonathan's body was rigid with tension. Carnegie's eyes were locked on his, and he could see the hatred simmering within them. He knew that if he looked away he was dead, so he stayed still, despite every muscle in his body screaming at him to run. They faced off against each other for a few seconds that felt like an eternity, before the wereman bellowed with fury and threw Grimshaw aside. The ringmaster was left scrabbling around on the flagstones, whimpering pathetically.

Carnegie stormed off into the night, growling and muttering furiously to himself. He lashed out at walls, streetlamps, a passing alley cat, and shot murderous glances back at the boys. Jonathan and Ricky followed several paces behind him, making sure that they kept their distance. After an extremely tense few minutes the snarls began to subside, his muscles stopped straining to break free from their clothing, and his spine sank back to its disheveled human position. Eventually he walked over to Jonathan and placed a hand on his shoulder, drawing him away from Ricky.

"How are you holding up?"

"I'm OK. My foot hurts a bit. My side hurts even more. And I lost my knife. But I'm alive."

"That's the spirit." Carnegie paused. "I didn't kill Skeet," he muttered.

"What?"

"Just so you know. I didn't kill him. He's not in good shape right now, but he's still alive."

Jonathan stared at him. "Why are you telling me this?"

"Because I would have killed Grimshaw back there. I might even have killed you. You took a lot of risks for that piece of slime."

"Perhaps. Maybe I've got more faith in you than you have."

Carnegie chuckled wryly. "Maybe you do. Come on. I'm still going to need some supper."

# 21

At the other end of Darkside, the fog descended on Savage Row like a cold, dank curtain. From the drawing room of Vendetta Heights, the maidservant Raquella watched as the great elm trees and gaunt iron railings on the edge of the estate slowly disappeared from view. The milky lights from the avenue streetlamps couldn't pierce the swirling gloom, and only served to cast the scene in a ghostly hue.

Though Raquella could never say that she felt exactly safe inside Vendetta Heights, at this moment in time she was glad to be inside. The drawing room was illuminated by paraffin lamps and a blazing fire that crackled and spat in the hearth. Her master had retired to his study several hours ago, leaving her free for the moment. Vendetta had been in a strange, erratic mood for the past couple of days. He had bellowed at Raquella over her serving of his lunch, only to mournfully apologize to her afterward. Such mood swings were unusual for him. They made her nervous, and she was glad when he left her alone.

Whatever it was that had affected her master so badly, Raquella suspected that it had something to do with Carnegie and the boy named Jonathan. Even now, she couldn't quite explain why she had not told Vendetta that the boy was lying about his name. There was just something about Jonathan, a mixture of vulnerability and inner strength that had made her want to help him. *And now,* she thought grimly to herself, *you're probably going to pay for it. If Vendetta ever finds out* . . . Despite the heat in the room, Raquella shivered. She knew what happened to those who crossed her master.

It had been nearly three years since his carriage had pulled up outside her house in a poor part of Darkside called the Lower Fleet. No one in the area had ever seen such an expensive vehicle before, and grimy children ran up to touch the engraved woodwork and press their faces up against the glass. The oldest of six children, Raquella had been busy bathing her younger sister, her sleeves rolled up and soapsuds stuck to her nose. She was unaware of what was happening until her parents called her downstairs, where Vendetta stood grandly in the hallway. His blue eyes scanned the surroundings, mercilessly registering every stain and tear, every broken piece of furniture. His light, elegant features had settled into an amused sneer.

Visibly shocked by such an important visitor gracing their house, Raquella's parents stammered out an explanation.

"Mr. Vendetta here needs a new serving maid."

"And he thinks that you should work for him!"

"Heavens to be. Isn't that wonderful news, Raquella?"

Briskly doing up the cuffs on her sleeves, she didn't bother to look up. "I suppose. How much does the job pay?"

Her mother gasped. "Raquella! You can't speak to Mr. Vendetta that way. I'm so sorry, sir. My eldest suffers from a quick mouth."

The banker waved away her apologies. "It is not a problem. The girl has ambition and greed — not necessarily bad characteristics."

Raquella returned Vendetta's appraising stare. "I have neither. Just a lot of brothers and sisters to support."

There was a long, cold pause.

"You know that working at the Heights poses

certain . . . hazards. Serving girls with quick mouths may encounter difficulties."

Raquella knew well enough. Rumors of death and disappearance on Savage Row filtered down to even the most run-down and crowded houses on the Lower Fleet. But her father was struggling to find work, and their meals were getting smaller and smaller. What choice did she have?

"If you are good enough to employ me, I will do everything I can to earn your favor."

His mouth twisted into a slight smile. "Maybe we shall get along, after all."

And in a way, they did. There were still times when Raquella spoke before thinking, the fires of hatred would blaze in her master's eyes, and her life hung in the balance. But she had survived his punishments, and her monthly pay enabled her to improve her family's lot. Vendetta valued her attentive service and quick thinking enough to keep her alive, and on occasion even confided in her. Still, Raquella found it hard to be grateful that she had been ripped away from her home to serve this cold, merciless killer. Maybe that was why she had helped Jonathan. Maybe it had nothing to do with him or Carnegie. Maybe she just wanted to punish Vendetta.

In the hearth a cinder popped loudly, making Raquella jump. She had been daydreaming for too long. There was still the silver to polish before tea could be served. She was about to move away from the window, but a noise from outside made her turn back. A carriage came careening out of the fog, the horse foaming at the mouth as it galloped at full speed up the driveway. As the carriage reached Vendetta Heights the driver suddenly hauled back on the reins, bringing the carriage to a juddering halt. The horse whinnied in protest and stamped its feet, steam rising from its body. The driver got down awkwardly from the carriage. Swathed in a long dark cloak, and hobbling badly, the driver ascended the steps to the front of the house with great difficulty and banged loudly on the door.

With her heart beating a little more quickly, Raquella walked briskly around to the front door and pulled it open. She had learned long ago with Vendetta's visitors that appearing confident was crucial, no matter how she felt on the inside. If they sensed that you were scared of them, you were in real trouble.

"Yes?" she said to the cloaked figure, a hint of imperiousness in her voice.

"I need to see Vendetta," the figure whispered.

"I'm afraid my master is indisposed at present. Perhaps I can take a message?"

The figure wearily pulled down its hood. Raquella started. It was Marianne. Her face was covered in cuts and gashes, and there were streaks of blood across her cheek.

"I haven't got time for this, Raquella," she said. "I have to see him now. It's urgent. Believe me, he'll want to see me."

Raquella opened the door wider and ushered the bounty hunter inside. She was taking a risk disturbing Vendetta, she knew, but Marianne's reason for visiting must be important if she was out in this condition. She gestured for Marianne to wait in the hallway, before heading over to the study.

Vendetta was asleep in one of the great armchairs, his face paler than usual. He jerked awake when Raquella timidly approached him, and gave her a baleful stare. "What is it?"

"I'm sorry to disturb you, sir, but Marianne is here. She says it's vital that she speaks to you."

Vendetta shifted in his chair with interest. "Well, well, well. You'd better send her in, then."

"Yes, sir."

Raquella curtsied and hurried back out into the

hallway, where Marianne was waiting impatiently. "About time," she muttered, nearly pushing past the serving maid as she was led to the study.

With Marianne inside the room, the house settled back into silence. Raquella stood still for a second, thinking furiously. Then she raced for the back staircase that the servants used. Lifting her skirt up away from her ankles, she took the stairs two at a time, coming out on the third floor. Here most of the rooms were disused, and Raquella treaded cautiously through the dark, her feet padding on the soft carpet. Pieces of furniture were muffled beneath thick sheets to protect them from dust, creating an eerie army of strangely shaped white objects.

In the last room a heavy door was set into the far wall. Retrieving a set of keys from her pocket, Raquella flicked through them looking for the right one. She noticed that her hands were shaking ever so slightly, and she sternly told herself not to be so silly. Then the correct key was in her hand, the door was open, and she had eased silently through into the room beyond.

Raquella knew this wooden balcony looked down into Vendetta's study. From this height, the room was even more impressive. Bookshelves filled every wall, stretching up to the ceiling until only the tallest ladders could reach them. On her hands and knees, Raquella crept forward to the edge of the balcony and peered through the wooden slats. Vendetta was standing in front of the fire, his arms folded behind his back, his shadow flung across the entire length of the room. Marianne sat in one of the armchairs, her face etched with exhaustion. For a time neither of them spoke, until Vendetta's calm, mocking voice cut in.

"Rough day?" he asked innocently.

Marianne shook her head. "Had an argument with a pool full of barracudas. Pandemonium broke loose at the Beastilia. Skeet has disappeared. I nearly lost Humble. He's being attended to now, but I don't know if he's going to pull through."

"My commiserations. What happened?"

"It was the boy. The Starling boy."

Raquella gasped quietly. By the fire, Vendetta started at the mention of the name. "You know where he is?"

"I know where he *was*. We had managed to take him to Grimshaw, but somehow he escaped. He took the other boy with him."

Vendetta smiled thinly, and wandered over to the drinks cabinet. He poured himself a measure of thick dark liquid from a crystal decanter and took a deep swig. A hint of color returned to his cheeks. "I would very much like to get my hands on that boy."

"Well," Marianne continued, "you could just ask Carnegie."

He whirled around. "What?"

"Carnegie. The detective. He's been protecting the boy since he crossed to Darkside. Didn't you know?"

Vendetta placed his glass down on the cabinet, his hands shaking with silent fury. "No. I didn't know that," he replied, in a voice that was awful in its stillness. The shadows lengthened in the room. "If you've held onto this information, you must have a reason." Vendetta leaned toward Marianne. "Why are you telling me this now?"

Marianne shrugged. "I need Skeet to track the boy. I need Humble's help to catch him. I don't have either of them right now. That boy has hurt two of my associates, and put me out of business — for now. So I thought I'd come and tell you all about it. And also, to give you something I found in the Beastilia."

She reached inside the folds of her cloak, wincing at an injury as she did so. Then she drew out a small item. Raquella leaned forward to see what it was, still terrified that she could be spotted at any moment.

She needn't have worried. Vendetta's eyes were transfixed on the slender dagger balanced on Marianne's bloodied palm. "Are we even now?" said the bounty hunter.

Vendetta snatched the dagger from her grasp, and retreated back into a huddle in the corner of the room, murmuring under his breath as he cradled and stroked his treasure. Marianne looked on in shock, and shrank back into her chair. Vendetta, always sophisticated and urbane, had been replaced by something like an animal. Eventually he rose and placed the dagger inside his waistcoat. Regaining his unruffled bearing, Vendetta smiled, and stroked Marianne's trembling cheek.

"For this, I am grateful. You will be rewarded."

"What now?" she whispered. "Are you going to hurt the Starling boy?"

"*Hurt* him? He has tried to cross me, Marianne — he's going to die. But not before he learns the real meaning of pain. Not before I pay his father a visit."

Raquella drew swiftly and silently away from the balcony. There was no time to waste.

# 22

Carnegie tossed another log on the fire, and let out a long sigh. He settled deeper into the chair, bathing in the warmth of the glow. Firelight flickered over the cuts on his face: sharp reminders of his struggle with Skeet. The animal rage had drained from his face, the bristles had receded, and the claws retracted. Now he looked wearier and more human than he ever had before.

By contrast, even in the relative safety of Carnegie's office, Ricky was struggling to calm down. He sat bolt upright, his head flicking around at the slightest sound, his body flinching with every scream that echoed up from Fitzwilliam Street. Jonathan knew how he felt. Adrenaline was still coursing through his veins. He hadn't stopped running and fighting since he had crossed over to Darkside, but he had never felt more alive. For the first time in his life, Jonathan didn't feel afraid of anything. Even so, for Ricky's sake, he went over to the window and drew the curtains closed.

"What do we do now, Carnegie?"

"Now? We rest," the wereman mumbled. "Send Ricky back to Lightside. Then I try to come up with a plan that means Vendetta doesn't kill us both."

"He won't come after you — not tonight anyway."

Jonathan whirled around. Raquella was standing in the doorway, a grave look on her face. Carnegie rose from his chair, rubbing his face drowsily.

"Raquella! What are you doing here?"

"I had to talk to you."

"If Vendetta finds out you've come here, you'll be in serious trouble, my dear."

She shook her head. "I had no choice. You don't have a phone. Anyway, he won't find out. He's gone to Lightside to feed. He's got his dagger back."

"I don't understand. What dagger?"

Raquella unbuttoned her cloak and sat down on the couch. "When he feeds on humans, Vendetta uses a dagger to slice them open. It's made of a rare substance that stops his victims passing on any diseases to him. He's always been paranoid that he'll pick up something nasty. Dirty blood — it's what kills most vampires in the end."

Slowly things started to become a little clearer for Jonathan. "Hang on a sec. I had that knife! I found it in the room next to my dad's at the hospital!"

Raquella nodded. "He must have made the link to you. That's why he's been chasing after you. His dagger is the key to his panic — without it, he couldn't feed. And tonight Marianne came to the house and returned it to him."

"But it was in my dad's ward. In London. On Lightside!"

"That's where he feeds sometimes. He can't drink pure Lightside blood — it's too potent; it would send him insane. But if people there have a bit of Darkside in their bloodstream, or seeping into their brain, he can drink it. It's one of the things that makes him so powerful. I guess the patients on your dad's ward must have associations with Darkside."

Jonathan was beginning to make a connection — and

then stopped in his tracks. "So what's he going to do now that he's got his dagger?"

He knew the answer to his own question. Raquella looked away. "He's traveling back to the hospital tonight. To feed again. And he knows your dad's there. Jonathan, I'm so sorry."

The room began to spin. Jonathan staggered, and then sat down sharply. Carnegie was trying to speak to him, but the words washed over him in a meaningless jumble. Vendetta was going to attack Alain, who was lying helpless in a hospital bed. The image of his dad lit a fire in Jonathan's chest.

"I have to get back to the hospital now!"

"He's got a head start on you. You won't be able to catch him."

"Then we have to warn him. There must be a way that we can get hold of him!"

Carnegie shook his head. "I'm sorry, boy. But we can't contact Lightside from here."

There was a small cough from the other side of the room. "I'm not sure," said Raquella dubiously, "but I think there might be a way. You remember the phone in

Vendetta's greenhouse? I overheard him speaking on it once, and I think he's managed to connect it to Lightside. He has so many contacts there, it would make sense. We could try and phone from there, if you like."

Carnegie punched one hand into the palm of another. "We'll have to give it a try. Throw me the hat, boy, and we'll get moving."

Throughout the conversation, Ricky had looked on the point of fainting. At the prospect of traveling to Vendetta Heights, he began to physically shake. "But if this guy's some kind of vampire . . . what happens if he catches us?"

"He's not there," Jonathan replied. "So he won't catch us."

"Can't I stay here anyway?" he pleaded.

Carnegie nodded. "If you want, boy. I suppose you might make it through the night."

There was another scream from outside. Ricky's face hardened. "I'll come with you."

The burly wereman patted him on the back. "Good lad. Knew you'd make the right decision."

There was a strange-looking vehicle parked outside Carnegie's rooms. It looked like a large carriage, but instead of horses there was simply an extended front section and an upright steering wheel rising starkly from the driver's seat.

"Vendetta's car," Raquella explained. "I borrowed it."

"You can drive it?"

"I can make it go. The rest sort of takes care of itself."

She hoisted herself up into the vehicle, and carefully rearranged her skirt before sitting down in the driver's seat. Jonathan and Ricky clambered up to the backseats, while Carnegie went around to the front of the car and began turning a handle in the grille of the machine.

Jonathan leaned forward and spoke into Raquella's ear. "You have to wind this thing up to make it go?"

With a splutter and a loud cracking noise the engine burst into life, sending the occupants of the car rattling around in their seats. Raquella turned around and glared at Jonathan. "There's no time to waste, and this is the fastest vehicle in Darkside," she snapped. "You can walk if you want."

Carnegie leaped up into the car, and she pulled away into the road with a screech and a loud blast on the horn.

It was a journey that Jonathan would never forget. They couldn't have been moving that quickly, but the fact that the vehicle had no sides or doors left them horribly exposed. They had to cling on for dear life to avoid being thrown onto the road. Beside him Ricky shuddered and bounced, and the pair of them banged into each other with every slight adjustment of the steering wheel. As the wind sliced through his hair and the cobblestones rumbled beneath him, Jonathan couldn't help but grin with exhilaration.

As usual on a Darkside night, the streets were filled with cabs and carriages and scampering urchins, but Raquella took no notice of them. With only her horn to protect her, she drove in a straight line irrespective of any oncoming traffic, and regardless of the shouts of surprise and curses from other drivers.

They hurtled down the Grand, past the bejeweled, well-to-do Darksiders heading into Kinski's Theater of the Macabre, the blood-drenched couples arguing outside Casino Sanguino, and the lonely, shadowy figures that haunted the doorways of the Psychosis Club. Jonathan counted at least three carriages that were forced to veer off the road and onto the sidewalk to avoid a collision with the car. Horses bucked and whinnied in fear. Chaos enveloped the road, but the one constant was the proud, insistent beeping of Vendetta's horn.

In the front seat, Carnegie looked ill at ease. He winced at every near miss, and flung a hand over his eyes when Raquella shaved the side of a horse-drawn bus. At one point he turned to her and bellowed, "You're going to kill us! Do you always drive like this?"

She replied without taking her eyes off the road. "I did on the journey here. I've never driven before today."

Carnegie groaned and placed his head in his hands.

The car shot off the Grand and began the gradual ascent up to Savage Row. The road was quieter now, the air a little fresher, and the leaves in the trees were dappled with moonlight. Behind them, the daunting silhouette of Darkside's factories and chimneys seemed to take a pace back.

Before too long the gothic outline of Vendetta Heights came into view. The gates were open, and the car flew up the gravel driveway. As they passed the fountain of the crying child, Raquella hit the brakes, and sent the car skidding to a standstill outside the front entrance. The engine pinged, and water ran across the hood like per-spiration. Jonathan's body felt shaky after the violent jolting of the journey, and he nearly fell over trying to get out of the vehicle.

Raquella's face was blackened with grime, but she was grinning from ear to ear. "Not a bad journey, eh? I'm definitely getting better."

Carnegie dismounted slowly. "Young lady, you are never driving again. Ever."

She pouted, and walked up the front steps of the house.

Inside, everything was pitch-black. Raquella lit a candle by the front door and began to walk softly through the hallway. The light cast skittish shadows on the paneled walls and grotesque artwork.

"Will anyone be here?" whispered Ricky.

"Shouldn't be. The cook will have gone home by now, and I'm the only servant who'll stay in this place at night."

They crept in silence through the house and out the back door toward the greenhouse. Here the fog was thickening, taking on a life of its own. Rain was mixed in with it, leaving sheens of water droplets across their faces. Jonathan's muscles were bunched in a tight knot, and with every step he became more convinced that there were evil creatures lurking somewhere beyond his line of sight. Beside him, Ricky felt, if anything, even more nervous than he had at the Beastilia Exotica. At least there he knew what he was up against. He wondered if he was ever going to see his home again.

In contrast to the house, the greenhouse was warm and welcoming. The stream trickled calmly, and the plants rustled softly as Jonathan moved past them. The phone was where he remembered it, on a table at the edge of the patio. Instead of a numberpad, it had a small wheel dotted with holes for each number.

"Every time you put a finger in a hole, you have to turn the wheel," explained Raquella, with exasperation. "Honestly, I thought you Lightsiders had lots of telephones."

He ignored her and wondered who to call. He didn't know the number for the hospital and he didn't have any friends, which left only one number. He put his finger in the first hole and began to dial.

The line was awful, but after what seemed like an age, a faint ring tone started up. Jonathan clutched the table. This was his only hope.

"Hello?"

"Mrs. Elwood. It's me! Jonathan!"

"Jonathan? Where are you? Are you all right?"

"I'm fine! Listen, it's Dad that's in trouble! You've got to help him!"

"What, dear? This is a dreadful line. You'll have to speak up!"

"Help Dad!" Jonathan shouted. "He's in danger!"

"Help who?"

From behind him, there was a roar from Carnegie, and then the line went dead.

# 23

Jonathan dropped the receiver and whirled around. Through the window of the greenhouse, he could see that the world outside had changed, and that the white pallor of the streetlamps through the fog had deepened into an impenetrable wall of black. "What's going on?" he cried.

There was a thump against the glass, as if something had been thrown against the building. Carnegie strode over to Raquella and grabbed her by the arm. His muscles were starting to flex and ripple underneath his suit, and the first few tufts of hair were sprouting out from his cheeks.

"Does Vendetta know we're here?" he growled thickly. "Did he order you to bring us here?"

"I don't know!" sobbed Raquella. "I didn't tell him anything! He must have set a guard before he left!"

There was another bang, louder than before, and then another. Above the thumps, Jonathan could make out a rippling, chattering noise.

"What is going on? What's outside?"

Carnegie glared at Raquella, and then let go of her suddenly. "Bats," he said. "Lots of them."

Jonathan raced over to the window, dragging over a paraffin lamp from the patio table. As he neared the glass, he could make out the vast, writhing beasts that made up the unholy congregation. Their wings beat furiously in the air and against one another. Heedless of their own safety, they flew headlong against the greenhouse in an attempt to force their way inside. He held the lamp up for a closer look and they shied away, baring tiny, needlepoint fangs in anger.

Racing back to the patio, Jonathan placed the lamp back on the table. "Well, they don't like the light. What else can we use against them?"

"Don't crosses hurt them?" asked Ricky.

Carnegie narrowed his eyes. "How do you mean?"

"You know . . ." Ricky crossed one finger over the other in the shape of a crucifix. "A cross!"

"What's that supposed to do to them? Send them home crying?"

"OK," said Jonathan, "how are we going to get out of here?"

From the side of the building there came the sound of splintering glass.

"They're breaking through!" screamed Ricky.

Carnegie roared with frustration and brought his fist down on the table, crumbling it into pieces. His eyes were now bloodshot, and for a moment Jonathan feared that the wereman might turn against one of them. He knelt down beside Raquella, who was sniffing quietly to herself. "We have to get out," he said softly. "Is there another way out?"

She nodded, and pointed away into the undergrowth. "Somewhere toward the back there. But I don't know exactly where. . . ."

There was an almighty crash as one of the windows finally succumbed to the huge pressure and shattered. The black, chirping crowd of enormous Darkside bats began to swarm into the building.

"Move!" screamed Jonathan. "Take any lamps you can!"

He hauled Raquella up onto her feet and began to drag her in the direction she had pointed. Ricky dashed to the other side of the patio and grabbed another lantern, and then headed after them. Before they plunged into the undergrowth Jonathan risked a glance behind him. As Carnegie's rage grew, his animal self took over, howling and tearing at his clothes. The bat swarm wasn't attacking him, but circled above in a giant arc, seeming to recognize a fellow creature of the night.

"CARNEGIE! COME ON!" Jonathan bellowed.

The wereman howled again, and then sprinted toward him.

They ran blindly through the plant life, stumbling over vines and roots. The vegetation closed in over their heads, forming a lush, impenetrable roof, and forcing the bats to funnel down the narrow path after them. The sound of their high-pitched squeals was deafening. Over his shoulder Jonathan could hear Carnegie's grunts, could feel his hot breath on the back of his neck, and he wasn't entirely sure whether the wereman was following him or chasing after him. Behind them, the dark tidal wave was flooding into the greenhouse. A lone bat managed to break through the tree cover, swooping down from the roof like a dive-bomber to claw at Raquella. She screamed and tried to knock the beast away. Jonathan lunged across her and swung the lamp at the bat, which recoiled from the light in horror. He swung again and caught it on the wing, sending it spinning into the bushes.

"Come on! They're gaining on us!" cried Ricky.

Despite his aching legs and the burning pain in his chest, Jonathan forced himself to run faster. Abruptly the twisting path came out in a small clearing. They had reached the far end of the greenhouse, and in front of them stood a rusty iron door covered in creepers. Ricky raced over and tried the handle.

"It's all rusted over. It won't budge!"

"Jonathan!" Raquella screamed, and suddenly there was a blizzard of bats around them, snapping and tearing at them all. Jonathan wrapped a protective arm around Raquella and swung the lantern around his head. He felt a sharp pain in the back of his head and realized that he had been caught by a claw.

"Do something, Carnegie!"

There was a roar in response, and the wereman flew past them, hurling himself at the door. It popped open like a champagne cork, and the freezing, damp fog began to seep into the greenhouse. Then Carnegie was beside him, his fur matted with blood.

"Ricky!" Jonathan shouted.

The bats had driven Ricky away from the door, and the boy was fighting for his life. He wielded his lantern like a weapon, thrusting sword-strokes of light into the writhing cloud of black.

Carnegie pulled a bottle from his inside pocket and grinned wolfishly at Jonathan.

"I'll get him. Move!" he growled.

Jonathan didn't need telling twice. Keeping his head ducked low to avoid any more blows, he raced for the freedom of the outdoors. Despite the lantern, it was impossible to see much through the billowing fog, and he and Raquella ran in haphazard directions, first left and then right — anything to take them farther away from the greenhouse. Beneath their feet the surface changed from stone to grass, and suddenly it became difficult for them to keep their footing on the slick lawn.

Another roar made Jonathan look behind him. He saw the faint glow of Ricky's lantern outside on the terrace, and watched as it was thrown in a graceful arc back through the window of the greenhouse. For a second nothing happened, and then there was a whooshing sound, and an explosion that tore through the mist and ripped the sky apart with flames. A vast, collective squeal of pain carried through the air, the sound of hundreds of vampire bats on fire. They were hurled across the sky like fragments of comets before crash-landing onto the earth.

Jonathan bent over double, in a vain attempt to catch his breath.

"What the heck was that?" Raquella panted.

"Carnegie's Special Recipe." He laughed. "He never goes anywhere without it."

"He did that with a *hip flask*?"

"I'll tell you another time." He cupped his hands and shouted at the top of his voice, expecting the big man to come out at any moment. "Carnegie?"

There was no reply.

"Ricky? Where are you?"

Silence.

"Carnegie! Come on. We're over here!"

The mist remained mute.

"Jonathan . . ." Raquella said gently.

"We have to find them!"

"How? We can't see anything. We have to keep going."

"No! They saved our lives!" Jonathan cried. Tears welled up in his eyes, but then Raquella gave his hand a fierce squeeze.

"We haven't got time for this. Do you want to reach your dad before Vendetta does? They'll be all right. Come on! That looks like a path. If I'm right, it'll take us to the back gate."

And with that they were moving again. Time seemed to stand still as they walked through the strange mist. All Jonathan could do was focus on each individual step, and make sure that he stayed on the path. He kept listening for a howl or a shout — any sign that Carnegie and Ricky had survived — but there was nothing.

Just when he thought that he couldn't take a step further, a set of ornate gates appeared in front of him like a mirage.

"We're here. This is the back gate."

She walked forward and pushed at the railings, which creaked painfully open. They walked out onto another wide, leafy avenue. Raquella shivered and wrapped her cloak tightly around her. "What now, Jonathan?"

"I have to get back to London, to Lightside. My dad's in danger. Where's the closest crossing point from here?"

Raquella looked at him doubtfully. "I only know of one that's within walking distance. It won't be easy, though."

Jonathan shrugged. "What is?"

# 24

The streets were deserted, and the sound of Raquella's heels clicking on the pavement echoed around the great houses of Savage Row. Twice Jonathan — convinced that he could hear footsteps nearby — dragged Raquella into the shelter of the nearest driveway and crouched behind the wall. No one ever appeared out of the fog, and after the third time she told him that the weather was playing tricks on his senses. He wasn't so sure. In Darkside, there was *always* something out there.

Eventually Raquella stopped and pointed. Ahead of them the broad avenue ran onto a smaller street, and on the corner of the intersection there was a small, circular building that reminded Jonathan of an observatory. A murky light shone through the glass dome on top of the building, illuminating a sign that read SAVAGE ROW.

"What's that?"

"It's the Savage Row tube station."

Jonathan's eye widened. "Tube station?"

"Yes. On the Dark Line."

"Darkside has a tube line?"

"We're not *quite* as backward as you think we are. It would take ages to get up to Bleakmoor otherwise."

"Bleakmoor? That sounds like a laugh."

She laughed. "Once this is all over, I'll take you up there. You'd have to see it to believe it."

Raquella strode up to the building and passed through the heavy revolving door. The area beyond was a large circular room that looked like a posh hotel lobby. There were comfortable armchairs, thick rugs on the floor, and potted plants. Beyond, a gleaming brass turnstile guarded a doorway marked TO THE TRAINS. Flaming torches lined the wall, lighting the room with a warm glow. Jonathan let out a low whistle.

"Very nice."

"Well, this is Savage Row. Not all the stations in Darkside are as nice as this one."

"I can imagine. A bit quiet though, isn't it?"

Raquella glanced around the deserted room. "Yes, well . . . the Dark Line has a pretty bad reputation. Not many people use it."

"A bad reputation in Darkside? What exactly goes on around here?"

"Oh, stop fussing. I told you, this is the quickest way you're going to get home."

She moved neatly past the furniture and dropped a small silver coin through a slot in the turnstile, then pushed through it. On the other side, she fished out another coin from her purse and tossed it to Jonathan.

"I don't suppose you have farthings in your part of London, do you?"

"What's a farthing?" he replied, and followed her through the turnstile.

The doorway led to a steep flight of stairs. Water seeped through cracks in the stonework above their heads, dribbling down the backs of their necks and making the steps treacherously slippery. Jonathan lifted a large torch from the wall and tried to light their way as best he could. They made slow, careful progress; Raquella clung to his arm as they went. As they descended deeper and deeper into the earth, the temperature became colder and colder, and before long Jonathan could make out the white wisps of his breath on the air.

"It was much nicer upstairs," he grumbled.

Raquella was too busy concentrating on where to place her feet to make any sharp replies.

Finally they reached the bottom of the stairs, and came out into an enormous underground cavern. Two platforms were separated by railway tracks, a wrought-iron bridge allowed passengers to cross from one side to the other. After the awkward descent Jonathan was surprised to see that the surroundings down here were as plush as they had been upstairs. The floor was smooth and marbled, and the ceiling had been painted and covered with intricate decorations. There were chairs and tables for passengers to use while they waited for the train. At that moment in time, they were all unoccupied. The only sound was the ominous ticking of the huge gothic clock on the wall, which read quarter past two. So much had happened that it felt like a year had passed since Alain had fallen ill again, rather than a couple of days.

Raquella peered up the track for any sight of a train. "One should be coming in a minute," she said. "They're pretty frequent this time of night."

"Where are we going to?"

"Vendetta once told me that there's a couple of places where the Darkline brushes against your London Underground. This train goes past an old disused station called Down Street. If you can get there, you can make it back up to Lightside and get to the hospital."

"What — I can get a *train* back home?"

She shrugged. "Not exactly. You'll see when you get there."

"But it can't be that simple! There's loads of people who work on the Underground, drivers and workmen and stuff. Don't you think they'd notice if some strange ghost train kept going past?"

"What makes you think they don't?"

"But then they'd know about . . ."

He trailed off as Raquella arched an eyebrow. She chuckled. "You really have a lot to learn about this. Listen! The train's coming."

Jonathan could make out a faint huffing noise emanating from the tunnel, and a lone tendril of steam curled out from the darkness. The railway tracks began to quiver in anticipation as the sound of the engine began to get louder. Then, with a piercing blast of a whistle, a large black locomotive exploded into the station, its wheels clattering at breakneck speed. Somewhere in the front car the driver hit the brakes, and the train ground to an uneasy halt. The entire cavern was choked with thick smoke.

Each car was partitioned off into small compartments. As far as Jonathan could see, all of them were empty. He yanked open the nearest door and helped Raquella up inside. Inside the compartment was a row of three seats facing one another, and a shutter that led off to a connecting passage that ran throughout the train. He slammed the door shut behind them, and the train immediately pulled away from the station.

They sat in silence at first. Jonathan stared vacantly out of the window into the blackness. "This is really creepy. It's like we're the only people around here."

"We probably are. There's quite a few gangs who travel up and down the Dark Line robbing people, and everyone knows how rich this part of town is. Most people on Savage Row won't risk coming down here."

"Ah."

"Of course, it gets a lot busier down toward the Grand. At Fitzwilliam Street, you have to step over corpses to get onto the train." Raquella noticed Jonathan's worried glance and giggled. "It's all right, silly. We'll be getting off before then."

"Right. OK," he replied, feeling a little relieved.

She frowned. "Of course, the real danger would be if the tunnel caved in. That'd kill us for sure."

Jonathan rubbed a weary hand over his face and said nothing.

The train continued on its eerie journey, past Upper Croft Street and The Wells. Left alone with his thoughts, Jonathan could feel the tension rising inside of him. But Raquella was right — now was not the time to get distracted worrying about Carnegie and Ricky. He had to be focused. He was getting close to Lightside, to his part of the city, where there was cable television and computers, astronauts and pop stars. There was also his dad. And Vendetta.

Raquella tapped him on the arm, interrupting him. "You should get ready. The train will pass Down Street anytime now."

"You're not coming with me?"

She looked down at her feet, and shook her head. "I'm sorry, Jonathan, but I'm a Darksider. Not many of us can make the crossing to your part of the city. I'm going to head back to Vendetta Heights and see if I can find Carnegie."

"What will happen to you if . . ." Jonathan could barely bring himself to say the words. ". . . if I fail? If can't stop Vendetta, and he comes back?"

"I'm not sure. I'll have to tell him something about the greenhouse, at least. I'll be all right, though. He's been angry with me before, and I'm still here."

"How can you go back to that man? He's a murderer and a vampire!"

"What choice do I have?" She spread her hands. "There aren't many jobs that pay as well as this one. It means I can feed my family, Jonathan. What else am I supposed to do?"

A grim look settled on Jonathan's face. "I don't know. But I'll think of something."

Raquella glanced away, to hide the fact that she was smiling. "Look, you need to concentrate. We're nearly there!"

"Can't be that soon. We'll still going pretty quickly."

She looked slightly abashed. "Yes . . . there's a slight problem with that. This train goes *past* the Down Street platform. It doesn't actually stop."

"So how am I supposed to get off?"

"Jump."

Jonathan glanced at the steam tumbling past the window. "Are you crazy? Have you seen how fast we're going?"

"There's no other way. You have to jump."

"I'll kill myself! Why didn't you say anything sooner?"

"Because I knew you'd get angry!"

"And you were right! You're telling me this is how Vendetta gets across?"

"To be fair, you did say you wanted the quickest way back to Lightside."

He swore under his breath, and flung open the door of the compartment. Immediately a thick pall of soot and steam flew into the car. The smoky mixture burned his eyes and made them both cough. The train driver gave the horn another loud blast. Jonathan peered out into the tunnel, and saw the winding platform come into view. Pressing his feet against each side of the door frame, he braced himself for the jump. He was blinded by the steam, and deafened by the clanking of the train's wheels. Not for the first time that evening, he wondered if he was going to die.

"Jonathan!" Raquella suddenly blurted out.

He looked back at her.

"Good luck."

He nodded grimly, and then readied himself. The horn sounded again, and he could sense the train flying past the platform. There was no time to think about it, no time to turn back. With a defiant yell he sprang out of the train. For a few seconds there was nothing, only the void, and then he hit the platform with a sickening thud.

# 25

Jonathan lay still, covered in dust and dirt, moaning softly under his breath. The impact of the landing had reopened the wound that Carnegie had inflicted upon him, and there was a sharp pain in his left arm that made him wonder whether he had broken it. Eventually he was able to raise himself up into an awkward sitting position. His clothes were ripped, and there was a patch of blood on his knee. Coughing from all the dust in his lungs, Jonathan tried to move his arm, only succeeding in sending a shock wave of pain through his system that made him cry out loud.

Slowly his eyes began to adjust to the lack of light, and he could make out certain shapes and objects around him. It was clear that the platform at Down Street hadn't been used for many years. Dust covered the floor and the wooden benches like a blanket of gray snow. Water was dripping listlessly into a puddle somewhere. In the distance large rats scuttled noisily to and fro, dominant and assured in their own private kingdom. Even though Jonathan's nostrils had become accustomed to the stench of Darkside, the reeking odor of the platform still made him gag.

Still, in a strange way it was tempting just to sit with his back against the wall and drift off to sleep — anything to get away from the pain of bruises and broken bones, to escape from savage weremen and hungry vampires. The squeaking of the rats had a lulling effect on his weary mind. Jonathan felt his eyes beginning to droop. Just a few minutes' rest, and then he would be all right. Everything would be all right. . . .

The image of Alain lying on his hospital bed flashed through Jonathan's mind, waking him up as if a bucket of cold water had been flung in his face. If he was going to save his dad, he had to get out of here. Gritting his teeth and using his good arm as a prop, Jonathan forced himself upright. The movement set off another wave of pain, but this time he refused to cry out. The rats squeaked loudly at one another.

He staggered toward a group of corridors heading off in different directions. It seemed hard to believe that, many years beforehand, crowds of ordinary Londoners had hurried through these tunnels, going shopping or heading home after a long day at work. Then there would have been lights, a comforting hustle and bustle, people chatting and laughing. But now it was just him and the rats. At that moment, many feet beneath the surface of the city, Jonathan had never felt more alone.

He was beginning to despair about ever getting out of the station when he glanced down at the floor and saw a set of footprints leading off down one of the hallways. They looked fresh. *Someone* had been here recently — maybe a man working for the Underground. Jonathan shook his head. No. He knew who it had to be. Someone else who had made the jump from the Dark Line. Someone else who had risked his life in order to make the fastest crossing from Savage Row. Clearly Vendetta was desperate to feed. A new burst of energy overtook Jonathan, and he set off in the direction of the footsteps. At one point a yellow danger sign ordered people to KEEP OUT. Jonathan smiled grimly as he headed past it. That meant he had to be going in the right direction. As he climbed up the stairs, he came across more modern signs of life: a plastic bucket filled with murky water, a rusty wrench, and a workman's hard hat.

Then the stairs came out into an empty shop with boarded-up windows. The door facing him was ajar, allowing a bright orange sliver of streetlight into the room. Jonathan could hear the rumble of traffic — modern cars, not horses and carriages — from the street outside. He should have been elated, but he wasn't. Whoever had made those footprints had opened that door. It could only be one creature, and he had a head start on Jonathan.

The first thing that hit him as he stepped back out into London was the air. The thick clouds of smog that hung over Darkside were gone, and the atmosphere felt fresh and renewed in a way that it never had before. The chimneys and factories had been replaced by skyscrapers and massive advertising signs that pumped a dazzling light out into the night. Instead of rattling carriages, squadrons of taxis motored along the roads, ferrying people back to their homes. Everywhere he looked Jonathan saw human faces and modern clothes. The clubs and bars may have closed, but young people still stood around in groups, eating fast food and joking with one another. The air was filled with their laughter.

Although it was another world away, the sense of ever-present menace that had infected him in Darkside was hard to shake off. Jonathan still expected a gnarled hand to reach out from the throng for his throat, or a dagger to dart toward his face. He cut quickly through the crowds, his senses on overload. With his Darkside clothes in tatters and cuts and bruises all over his body, Jonathan knew that he looked a mess, but it didn't matter. He was back on the streets of London, the city he knew, this huge sprawl where nobody knew him and nobody cared. He was invisible again. Occasionally an adult caught sight of Jonathan and frowned in surprise, but he was gone before they could say anything. On the busier roads there were policemen dressed in high-visibility green jackets, and Jonathan made a particular point of staying out of their way. If they saw him they would stop him for sure and ask a host of questions that he didn't have time to answer.

After a twenty-minute sprint Jonathan raced panting through the grounds of St. Christopher's. It was quieter here, and only the presence of lights in a couple of windows suggested that anyone was awake at all. He dashed through the courtyard and reached the entrance to Alain's ward. Mercifully, the door wasn't locked. Upstairs, in the reception area, there was one nurse sitting quietly behind the desk, her face illuminated by a reading lamp. She was deeply engrossed in a stack of medical reports, and didn't notice Jonathan until he had nearly crept past her.

"Hey!" she called, but he was already running down the corridor. There wasn't time to argue, and anyway, the more security on their way to Alain's room the better.

He ran from memory now, cutting left and heading through one of the wards. The lights were off here and most of the patients were asleep. Jonathan could hear their troubled murmurs as they dreamed. In the background he heard another nurse shout with surprise, and then a loud alarm was echoing through the building. It woke up the patients in the next ward, and as Jonathan dashed through it, a small man with a wild look in his eyes set upon the patient in the bed next to him. The room disintegrated into a wild mess of fighting and screaming. Over his shoulder Jonathan could see the first wave of white-coated orderlies struggling to regain order. It was going to take them a long time.

Outside the ward he took a skiddy right turn, nearly slipping over on the slick surface of the linoleum. Then he was in his dad's hallway. Most of the rooms were locked, but at the end one door was open, and light streamed out from it into the hall. Jonathan's heart skipped a beat. It was his dad's room. No noise was coming from inside it. He stopped running and walked slowly toward it, sweat dripping down his forehead and his breath coming in snatches. There was nowhere to run — nowhere to hide now. In some detached part of his brain, Jonathan realized that he didn't have any sort of weapon. If Vendetta was in there, Jonathan would probably soon be as dead as his father. Clutching the door frame with his good arm, Jonathan looked inside.

The bulb above the bed cast a pool of light inside the room, and instantly he could make out the figure of Alain Starling stretched out in the bed, as if he hadn't moved since the last time Jonathan had been there. Next to him a man had pulled up one of the visitors' chairs on the far side of the bed, and was leaning in toward him.

"No!" cried Jonathan and rushed forward.

The man in the chair turned, revealing a round, friendly face with a startled expression, and Jonathan was stopped in his tracks.

"Jonathan?" the man said.

"Who are you? How do you know my name?"

The man flipped open his wallet, revealing an identification card. "My name is Officer Shaw. We've been looking for you, Jonathan. Everyone's been very worried."

"What are you doing here?" Jonathan asked suspiciously.

"We received a phone call tonight from a friend of yours. Mrs. Elwood. She said that you'd told her your dad was in danger. So . . ." He waved a hand around the room. "Here I am. I was just checking that he was breathing. I've never seen a coma like this before. Do you want to tell me what's going on, Jonathan?"

Jonathan felt his shoulders begin to relax. Mrs. Elwood had understood after all. His dad was safe. They were all safe. Suddenly he could feel his arm begin to throb again. Even so, he began to laugh. "I would, but you'd never believe me. It sounds crazy."

"Well, it's a crazy world," came a voice from behind him.

Jonathan whirled around. A figure was standing in the hallway, swathed in the shadows.

"Ah, Jonathan, this is my superior," said Officer Shaw. "Carter Roberts, head of the Special Investigations Unit."

The figure walked into the room, and Jonathan gasped. It was Vendetta.

# 26

Jonathan's head spun. He gasped and took a step back, pointing at Vendetta. By the bed, Officer Shaw was still talking.

"Mr. Starling's not responding to any stimulus, sir. Nurses say he's been like that for a couple of days. I can't see that he's in any immediate danger, though."

"It's him! He's the danger!" Jonathan shouted.

Shaw chuckled. "Now, Jonathan, I don't think you have to worry about Detective Roberts. He's a very senior police officer. He's been leading the investigation into your disappearance."

"But he's been trying to get me! And he's come here to kill my dad!"

"Actually, it was me that told Detective Roberts about your dad and asked him to come down here. You need to calm down, son. These sorts of crazy allegations don't help anyone."

Vendetta held up a hand to Shaw. "Don't worry about it, Officer. Seeing as I've been dragged out of bed to stand guard over a comatose patient, I'm happy to hear the boy out." He turned to Jonathan, smiling. "So . . . how exactly have I tried to 'get' you?"

"You were looking for your dagger that you cut people open with, so you sent Carnegie after me, but you didn't know that we were friends." He spoke breathlessly, the words tumbling out over and on top of one another. "But then you got the dagger and you came here to feed on my dad, but we found out and I managed to warn Mrs. Elwood and now I'm here so you can't do anything. . . ."

The look of bewilderment on Officer Shaw's face was enough to stop him in his tracks. "Listen, son," the policeman began sympathetically. "I know you've been through a lot but —"

"It's true!" Jonathan shouted. "I'm telling you, it's the truth! You have to believe me! He's a vampire!"

The room fell into silence. Then the sound of Vendetta's

mocking laughter filled the air. "You got me. Guilty as charged. I am a vampire. Dracula's great-grandson, or something like that."

"Sir, the kid's obviously had a rough few days. . . ."

"That's all right, Shaw. I've been called a lot worse." Vendetta reached out a hand toward Jonathan, who shrank away from him. "Look, Jonathan, you're badly injured. Someone needs to have a look at that arm — it looks like it's broken. Why don't you let us take care of you, and then you can tell Officer Shaw why I'm a vampire. He might even let you make a statement."

Jonathan edged back toward his dad's bedside. "Stay away from me, Vendetta. I'm not going anywhere."

The two men exchanged glances with each other. Officer Shaw sighed and rose out of his chair. "Come on, son. Now's not the time to be playing these sorts of games."

"It's not a game! My dad's life is in danger!"

Shaw skirted around the bed and advanced upon Jonathan. He kept his hands up in the air in a non-threatening gesture. "Once we've patched you up and you've had a rest you'll feel a lot better. Things'll seem different in the morning, I promise."

Jonathan looked around frantically for some kind of weapon he could use to ward off the policeman, but the room was bare.

"Come on. Let's go get a coffee or something."

Shaw reached out and clasped hold of his good arm. Jonathan squirmed frantically, but it was no use. He was down to his last reserves of strength, and the policeman was surprisingly strong. Although he was trying not to squeeze too tightly on Jonathan's arm, his grip was still as firm as a vise. He led Jonathan firmly toward the door, ignoring his squirming and shouting. Vendetta looked on with undisguised amusement. Tears of frustration sprang into Jonathan's eyes. He had come so far, and gotten so close, but it had all been for nothing.

"We'll talk back at the station when you've calmed down," said Vendetta. "I have a feeling we'll have a lot to talk about, don't you?"

Jonathan kicked out at him, missing by a foot or so. He gave Vendetta a vicious stare. "If you harm my dad, I'll kill you. Do you hear that? I'll kill you, and Marianne, and Grimshaw. ALL OF YOU!"

Shaw managed to drag him out of the room and slam the door behind them. The boy's shouts could still be heard echoing down the corridor as he was led away. Vendetta smiled, and turned to Alain Starling.

"Well, now. Looks like we're finally alone. I've been waiting to meet you for some time. I should congratulate you on your son. He's quite a remarkable boy. Not remarkable enough to save you, but still . . . most impressive. You're going to miss him."

And with that, he turned off the light.

The boy was running out of energy now. Shaw had managed to grab one of the orderlies and together the two of them bundled Jonathan back through the wards. At first he had struggled like a wildcat, but it was impossible to keep up the fight. Now he was close to admitting defeat; his kicks were weaker, and his head lolled wearily to one side.

By all accounts, Shaw should have felt elated. He had been personally responsible for the retrieval of one of the boys. Maybe Jonathan would be able to lead them to Ricky. The whole case could be sewn up within hours, and it would all be because of him. In a high-profile case such as this, a promotion would be a certainty. It would probably make his career. So why wasn't he happy? Why did he have this strange feeling that something was terribly wrong? Why was there a nagging voice at the back of his head telling him that he had missed something of great importance?

They had reached the reception desk. Soon they would be out of the hospital and heading for the police station. Jonathan had stopped moving altogether now, and he hung like a deadweight from the two men. Shaw knitted his brows together. *Think, man!* he told himself. *What have you missed?* The boy had cooked up such an unbelievable story that it was hard to imagine that there was a word of truth in it. Daggers and vampires, all those characters with ridiculous names . . .

And then, like that, there it was. Shaw stopped and urgently shook Jonathan.

"Who's Marianne?"

"What?"

"Marianne. You mentioned her back there. Who is she?"

Jonathan sighed wearily. "She's a bounty hunter who was hired to kidnap me and Ricky. She has fluorescent hair and two accomplices — a weird little bald guy and a giant who can run really quickly. She returned

Vendetta's dagger to him, and he's going to use it to kill my dad. Believe any of that?"

Suddenly the fog lifted from Shaw's mind, and everything fell into place: the photograph of Ricky in Trafalgar Square, the surveillance footage of the giant, the conversation Roberts had had with the biker in the lockup garage. It might have sounded insane, but the boy was telling the truth. A grim look descended onto Shaw's face.

"Every word, actually. Come on."

They rushed back to the room, only to find that the door was locked. Ushering Jonathan out of the way, Shaw took a running start and put his shoulder to it, bursting the door off its hinges. Inside the room he scrabbled for the light switch. Vendetta was crouched over Alain, the dagger raised above his head. He spun around at the commotion, and the policeman took a step back in horror. Where before had been the cool face of Carter Roberts, head of the Special Investigations Unit, now there was an angular, bestial mask of hatred. The color had drained from his face, his eyes had contracted into black slits, and sharp stained teeth protruded out from his lower lip. Beside Shaw, Jonathan offered up a silent prayer of thanks.

There was no blood on Vendetta's fangs — they had gotten here just in time.

Vendetta hissed with fury and stepped away from Alain. "I told you to take the boy out of here," he seethed, running a thick red tongue over his lips.

"He forgot to say good-bye to his dad," Shaw replied calmly.

"Another minute, and it would have been too late for that. Can't you do *anything* right?"

"Why don't you step away from the bed, sir . . . or whatever you are?"

Vendetta paused, calculating his next move. As he flexed his hands Jonathan stared at them in horrid fascination. The skin had aged until it looked like yellowed parchment, and the fingers were bony and elongated. Long dirty nails cut menacingly through the air.

"And if I don't?"

"Step away from the bed!"

The vampire didn't hesitate. With a snarl it leaped at Shaw, springing with incredible power. The policeman was caught off guard, and could only throw up his hands to protect his face as Vendetta crashed into him. The two of them fell, and rolled across the floor in a tangle of arms and legs. Jonathan saw a fist rise and come down again, heard a grunt of pain. Then something gleamed in the strip light, and he recognized the dagger. Jonathan hurled himself in a desperate dive toward it, but only succeeded in bouncing off Vendetta's fist. It felt like running headlong into a brick wall. His broken arm throbbed with pain.

The vampire spat with anger and hurled Shaw out of the way, sending the policeman flying onto the bed. Vendetta turned and went after Jonathan, blood dripping from his right hand. He held aloft the dagger and laughed thickly, and Jonathan knew that it was all over. The vampire grabbed him by the collar and whispered in his ear.

"After I've finished with you, I'm going to drain your father."

Jonathan swung a punch at his chest, but the vampire didn't even flinch. With one hand Vendetta pressed him against the wall, and with the other he sliced carefully down his neck with the dagger. Half-numb with terror, Jonathan could see the thin stream of red liquid running down the front of his clothes. Vendetta leaned in, and he could feel his freezing breath upon his neck. He closed his eyes and waited for the pain to end.

Everything stopped. There was a scream of anguish, but

it didn't come from Jonathan's mouth, and suddenly Vendetta had released his grip. Before Jonathan hit the floor in a heap, he saw an unfamiliar figure standing behind the vampire. Then he was dimly aware that someone had stumbled out of the door; Shaw was standing over him and the other man, and Jonathan realized that he did know who it was after all. Before he lost consciousness, the last thing he saw was his father.

# 27

Outside a police station in central London, the rain pattered gently down onto the journalists gathered around the front entrance. Some jabbered excitedly into their cell phones, while others scribbled their thoughts down on sodden notepads. Photographers checked their equipment settings against the lighting. Television correspondents practiced their pieces to the camera. Everywhere, there was the hum of expectation.

A policeman headed through the revolving doors and out onto the street. Immediately the journalists raced toward him, forming a scrum of microphones and flashbulbs. They all began shouting questions at once, until the policeman raised a hand for silence.

"I have a short statement to read out, and then I'll

take your questions." He cleared his throat and flattened out a piece of paper in his hand. "Last night police officers working in conjunction with the Special Investigations Unit were able to locate and rescue one of the two children snatched by a gang of kidnappers in the past week. The child is unharmed and has been reunited with his family. The perpetrators of this crime have yet to be apprehended. It is believed that they have fled the country. Nevertheless, the SIU is confident that the kidnapping ring has been permanently disabled, and that it poses no further threat to children here. Any questions?"

"Officer Shaw . . ." began one reporter.

"Sergeant Shaw," he corrected with a smile.

"Sorry, *Sergeant* Shaw. Could you tell us the name of the child the police have rescued?"

"Yes. His name is Ricky Thomas. He is doing very well and is glad to be back at home."

Sergeant Shaw glanced away. The reporter seized on the pause and piped up with another question. "We were expecting the SIU to have some comments on this case, but they are refusing to answer any questions. Is there any truth to the rumor that Detective Carter Roberts was removed from the case due to incompetence?"

"I can't comment on that. I can confirm that Mr. Roberts has resigned from the SIU with immediate effect."

"What about the other child?" The reporter glanced down at his notebook. "Jonathan Starling? Any clue as to his whereabouts?"

"At this precise moment in time we cannot locate him, though we are following up on several leads. I can assure the public that we will not give up until we have recovered the boy."

On the other side of the road, two figures looked on with amusement. One was a young teenager, his unruly brown hair rustling in the breeze. His arm was in a sling and his face was covered in cuts, but there was a smile on his face and he rested easily against a low stone wall. The other figure was a tall, hairy man wrapped up in a thick coat. A battered wide-brimmed hat was forced down over his head, and his eyes were full of distaste.

"That policeman's loving every second of this, isn't he?"

"Let him. If he hadn't listened to me, my dad would be dead."

The man growled. "I feel stupid in this hat. I don't see why I couldn't wear mine."

"You look stupid. But you're on my side of London now, so you have to do things my way. If you're going to be in a mood, Carnegie, you can go back to Darkside now."

"Don't tempt me. This place is weird." There was an awkward pause, and the wereman coughed. "I'm sorry I wasn't there. You know, in the ward."

"I'm just glad you're alive. I thought you and Ricky were goners."

"It must have been a particularly potent batch of my recipe. We were blown halfway across Vendetta Heights. I was surprised that Ricky was still in one piece. That boy's tougher than he looks. Even so, we couldn't get here in time."

"That's all right," Jonathan said happily. "My dad was there. So it was OK."

Carnegie shook his head. "Amazing the energy you can muster when someone's trying to eat your son."

"Well, I think Shaw being thrown on top of him might have had something to do with him waking up, but . . . yeah, I think amazing is the right word."

"How's Alain doing now?"

"Still pretty weak. He spends a lot of time sleeping. The doctors think he's going to be fine, though. Eventually. If he's got enough strength to beat Vendetta, he can't be that bad."

"Have you two had a chance to talk yet?"

Jonathan sighed. "Not really. He's too confused to get any real answers out of him. Just ends up mumbling nonsense."

"Give it time, boy. He'll come around."

"But he's had all this time to tell me . . . about my mother, I mean."

The wereman shuffled uncomfortably. "Don't be too hard on your dad. Alain's had a pretty rough time too, you know."

"All I know is he's been trying to get back to Darkside for years. If that's got something to do with Mom then I'm going to find out what, whether he tells me or not."

The press conference broke up, and the journalists raced away to file their stories. Sergeant Shaw stood on the steps of the police station on his own, still basking in the moment. Catching sight of the two figures on the other side of the road, he gave them a quick salute and a wink. Carnegie snorted, and led Jonathan away from the station and down a side street that curved toward the Thames.

"How did you get him to agree to that, then?"

"Agree to what?"

"Pretending that you're still missing. I'd have thought he would have looked even better if he could have paraded you in front of the cameras."

Jonathan laughed. "Not likely. I told him that I was going to tell the press everything — about Darkside, kidnappers, vampires working for the SIU. No way anyone was going to promote him then. So he turned a bit green and agreed that it might be best if I stayed underground for a bit. Everyone who cares about me knows I'm safe. And I don't really want to go back to school yet."

"Won't people miss you?"

"I'm invisible around here. They'll forget quickly enough."

Down by the waterfront, birds were circling idly on the wind currents. Tourists milled around, taking turns photographing one another. A juggler tossed pins higher and higher into the air, vainly trying to attract an audience. Carnegie leaned on a rail and stared out over the gray Thames.

"So you're free — for now. What are you going to do with your time?"

"Well . . ." Jonathan said, a hopeful note creeping

into his voice. "Dad's going to be fine, but it's not like I can visit him in the hospital. I am supposed to be missing, after all. And people would recognize me if I went to Mrs. Elwood's house. So I was thinking . . ."

"What?"

Jonathan gave him a beaming smile.

"No. Absolutely not. You must be kidding me!"

"It won't be for long!"

"You know that Vendetta will be there! He's not a man to forget a grudge. If you start wandering around Darkside he'll come after you. He's probably dreaming up ways to kill us both right now."

"I'm not scared of him. We've beaten him before. We can do it again."

"Bold words. I'm glad you're so confident. If you haven't forgotten, I'm a private detective, boy. I can't spend my time babysitting."

"I won't get in your way. I promise."

"How many times did you nearly die in Darkside?"

"That's why I need to go back there! I need to learn. Carnegie, I'm a Darksider too, remember. It's part of me!"

Carnegie turned and began hurrying away from the

river. Jonathan chased after him, skipping around the knots of tourists. "You could show me all the sights!"

"Sights? What sights?" the wereman called over his shoulder.

"Well . . . Raquella said she'd take me to Bleakmoor on the train."

"BLEAKMOOR!" Carnegie bellowed, causing a flock of pigeons to take to the air in alarm. "Have you any idea how dangerous that place is?"

"That's why I need you to come with me," Jonathan replied. "Otherwise, I'll be in all kinds of trouble."

Carnegie gave Jonathan a long, hard stare. Eventually he sighed, defeated, and ruffled Jonathan's hair.

"Come on, then, boy. If we're going to cross, we should cross now." He glanced up at the sky. "It'll be getting dark soon."

And now, an exclusive sneak preview from the fourth chapter of the next book in the **DARKSIDE** series...

# LIFEBLOOD

by Tom Becker

Arthur went over to the window and peered outside, before carefully closing the blinds. Satisfied that no one could see them talking, he settled himself down in a stiff-backed chair, which groaned under the weight. He spoke in a low voice, often pausing mid-sentence to glance around the office.

"To be honest, I stumbled across this by accident. I was down at Devil's Wharf, questioning one of the dockers about some decidedly fishy nighttime deliveries that were taking place around the Rafferty warehouses. As we were talking, word started flying around that a body had been found in the Lower Fleet. Seeing as I wasn't getting any useful information, I thought I'd take a chance on the scoop and see what I could find. Now I almost wished that I hadn't."

There was a haunting, lyrical quality to Arthur's voice. Jonathan found himself leaning in closer to listen to him. The clatter of the printing presses below them faded into a background hum.

"I was on the verge of giving up and going home when I came across a tiny alleyway in the middle of the Lower Fleet. Its contents were . . . not a pretty sight." He paused. "A man's body was lying in the middle of the alleyway. Or what was left of it — he looked like he'd been ripped apart by a pack of wild animals. The sight of it was nearly enough to make me sick.

"At that time there was no one else around. The alleyway looked derelict — there was no guarantee that anyone would come to claim the body or take it away. So once I'd caught my breath, I searched the body and tried to find out who the poor soul was."

The thought of rifling through the pockets of a dismembered corpse sent a shudder of revulsion down Jonathan's spine. By contrast, Carnegie's ears pricked up, and the bored expression on his face vanished.

"What did you find?"

"The usual stuff: loose change, matches, a bunch of keys. Nothing that could help us identify him."

Lucien leaned forward.

"Which is where you come in, Carnegie. We want you to help us find out who this man was, and what happened to him."

The wereman tapped his fingers together thoughtfully.

"Well, this is all very interesting, but before we talk business I need you to answer a question for me. People get murdered in Darkside all the time. You write up what happened, people buy your newspaper, life carries on. So stop messing around and tell me why you're taking so much trouble over this one!"

Suddenly his voice was as cold and hard as steel. Lucien and Arthur glanced at each other, and eventually the former nodded.

"Look," said Arthur, "I've spent the last few years of my life documenting murders and going over old case files. Of all the hundreds of corpses I've seen, only one body has ever looked the way this one did. And that was James Ripper."

The temperature in the room dropped by a couple of degrees. Carnegie sighed and rubbed his eyes, while Lucien bit a fingernail pensively. Arthur looked regretful for even having mentioned the name.

"Sorry, but who's James Ripper?" asked Jonathan.

"Good question," an amused voice answered from the doorway. "You should be a reporter."

A boy was leaning idly against the door frame, hands in his pockets. His sleeves were rolled up, and a couple of shirt buttons were left undone, in order to display as much of his muscular physique as possible. Despite looking the same age as Jonathan, he carried himself with an easy arrogance, and his voice dripped with condescension.

"Harry Pierce, I've told you a million times to knock before coming in here," Lucien said sharply. "This isn't a good time."

"Sorry, boss. But come on — he's got to be the only person in Darkside who doesn't know who James Ripper is."

"I'm not from around here," Jonathan shot back coldly.

"Well, let me fill you in," Harry said eagerly, pulling up a chair before anyone could stop him. "This is the most famous murder in the history of Darkside (and you'd better believe there's been a fair bit of competition for that title). Twelve years ago a guy was found dead on the roof of The Cain Club — and however he'd died, it hadn't been pretty. Anyway, word gets out that this isn't any old corpse, but the son of Thomas Ripper, grandson of Jack the Ripper and the current ruler of Darkside now — though for how much longer that old boy's going to stay around is another question. . . ."

"Harry!" Arthur warned.

"Right. Sorry, boss. Anyway, Thomas was so furious that he tore the place apart trying to find who was responsible, but the killer was never found. To this day, no one knows who would dare kill a Ripper, and — more important — why. Was it a random murder? Or had someone managed to find out that James was a Ripper before the Blood Succession?"

Jonathan's brain was drowning in the torrent of new information.

"Blood Succession? What's that?"

Harry laughed disbelievingly.

"Another searching question about the bleeding obvious. Is there anything you do know?"

"That'll do, Pierce," Lucien cut in. "I think you've graced us with enough of your presence for one day. And stop bloody eavesdropping!"

The young man bowed mockingly and withdrew.

"Sorry about that," Lucien said apologetically. "I should really fire that brat. Problem is, he's got the makings of a fine reporter. We can't afford to be picky around here. The staff gets smaller every day." He looked at Carnegie. "But you understand why we're taking this case so seriously. It may be nothing, but if there's even the slightest link to James's murder, then it's worth the effort. What do you say?"

"You know my usual rates?"

Lucien smiled.

"Your reputation precedes you. And I wouldn't dream of offering anything less."

Carnegie picked at his teeth with a claw, and spat something on the floor.

"You've got yourself a deal, then. Enough jabbering. Come on, boy, we need to go and find out who this guy is."

He placed a large hand on Jonathan's shoulder, and the two of them turned to go, with Arthur stomping along in their wake. From the other side of the office, Harry Pierce watched them leave, his eyes glinting in the candlelight.